The CUPID Company

First published in Great Britain by HarperCollins
Children's Books 2011
HarperCollins *Children's Books* is a division of
HarperCollins*Publishers* Ltd,
77–85 Fulham Palace Road, Hammersmith, London W6 8JB

Visit us on the web at
www.harpercollins.co.uk

1

THE CUPID COMPANY, Perfect Match
Text copyright © HarperCollins *Children's Books* 2011

Amber Aitken asserts the moral right to be identified
as the author of this work.

ISBN-13 978-0-00-736263-9

Typeset by Palimpsest Book Production Limited,
Falkirk, Stirlingshire

Printed and bound in England by
Clays Ltd, St Ives plc

Amber Aitken

The CUPID Company

Perfect Match

HarperCollins *Children's Books*

Also by Amber Aitken

The Cupid Company – It Takes Two
The Cupid Company – Heart to Heart
The Cupid Company – Forever and Ever

finders. losers

The trees along the seashore were flattened at the front and looked like a line of tall, thin ladies with their hair blown back. It was a very windy day, which was quite unusual. Sunday Harbour was definitely more of a calm, balmy sort of seaside town, especially during the summer. But then it was nearing the end of August, so there really wasn't very much of a summer left.

"I'll never manage to brush these knots out," grumbled Coral, whose right hand had disappeared in the mass of reddish-brown curls on her windswept head. Finally she gave up trying to batten down her hair. She extracted her hand and rolled her eyes back so that she could watch her crazy curls break-dancing in the wind.

"Mad, mad hair," she grumbled some more.

Sensible Nicks had plaited her long blonde hair so that it hung, neat and tidy, down her back. She was calmly flipping through some drawings in a box on a bare wooden table with a sign that spelled: *ALLY'S ARTWORKS*.

Every six weeks – no matter what the weather – the colourful tables of the seaside market made an appearance on the stretch of grass near the foreshore. These would be carried from the boots of nearby parked cars and unfolded in tidy, even rows. From these tables the people of Sunday Harbour (as well as some visitors from the next seaside town along) sold things like second-hand books, potted plants, freshly baked breads and pastries, clothes, arts and crafts, homemade jams and pickles, pottery, sweets and bric-a-brac. Everyone loved the seaside market; you would need a pretty good reason to stay away.

Suddenly Coral spied a table with a sign saying *GIFTS BY APHRODITE* and quickly made her way over. She wasn't in the market for a gift, but Aphrodite was the Greek goddess of love and there was not a lot that Coral loved more than love itself. It was the central theme in her life. Love was the reason for almost everything, including the Cupid Company. It had inspired Coral and Nicks to become matchmakers.

She surveyed the table with her hands on her hips, searching for a heart-shaped this or a heart-decorated that, but the table was mostly filled with painted clay dragons bejewelled with colourful bits of glued-on glass.

"Hello, I'm Aphrodite. Can I help you?" said the woman on the other side of the table.

Coral stared at the woman, who in turn stared up at Coral. And then Coral shrugged at the woman called Aphrodite who was definitely not the Greek goddess of love and sold dragons instead of hearts. Coral was just about to move on when Nicks suddenly appeared and squeezed up close beside her.

"I have a present for you, take a look," she said in a conspiratorial whisper, holding up a clenched fist to her friend.

Coral loved surprises and did not need to be told twice. Prising Nicks's fingers apart, she found her present – a hair band. But not just any hair band – one with a candy-pink, heart-shaped bobble attached. Coral grinned and in a matter of moments had her crazy curls tied up and bound with a heart. She laid an arm across Nicks's shoulders.

"You know, you really are the best friend a girl could have."

Nicks shrugged and nodded.

"Ooooh, look over there." Coral pointed to a table stacked with elaborate wigs on polystyrene heads. There were also trays of costume jewellery, old-fashioned leather shoes with big buckles and bows, colourful masks, pots of face paint, a few feather boas and a large silver shield. Beside the table stood a clothes rail that was heavy with hanging bits of bright, decorative material. A folded sign on the table explained it all: *SUNDAY HARBOUR THEATRE COMPANY.* The items were obviously from their prop cupboard and being sold to raise funds on their behalf.

Coral grabbed Nicks's cardigan and towed her over to the table. There was a red satin half-mask with feathers, nestled amongst the costume jewellery. She quickly scooped it up and pressed it to her eyes.

"How do I look?"

"Like you've got feathers growing out of your ears," replied Nicks.

Suddenly, a man with a curly moustache appeared from behind the clothes rail. "Oh, that is fabulous on you, girl!" He applauded Coral, who grinned and fluttered her eyelashes behind the mask.

Nicks made a 'mmm' sound and wandered over to the rail. The hanging clothes were colourful and detailed with delicate embroidery, rose ribbons, lace, fringing and sensational sequins – if you were into that sort of thing. And Coral clearly was. She quickly abandoned the mask and pounced on a vintage-style waistcoat in faded denim with silver piping. It had pockets and a neat row of pressed metal buttons featuring some sort of coat of arms. Coral eyed it up carefully. *This waistcoat is military meets high fashion*, she thought. She put it on and posed, hoping the man with the curly moustache might notice her fabulousness once again. But this time the man was very busy seeing to some other girl who had a white ringlet wig on her head.

"Oh, that is fabulous on you, girl!" cried the man once again.

Coral's eyes narrowed, but she was not put off. "I think I'll definitely take the waistcoat," she said to Nicks, choosing to ignore her friend's frown. "Waistcoats are fashion's key item for layering," she explained (just as she'd read in one of her mum's magazines).

Nicks smoothed her forehead and sighed. Experience had taught her that there was no point in arguing with her single-minded friend. "Well, give the man his money, Coral. The game of beach volleyball is starting up and I want to cheer on the Sunday Harbour Spikers. They just *have* to beat the Biscuit Bay Bombers!"

Of course Nicks was right. Everyone in Sunday Harbour supported their local volleyball team, and today was the semi-finals. The team that won today's game would go on to play the mighty Dune High Decoys in a few weeks' time. This tournament final was the main attraction at the *Farewell to Summer Beach Party*, but the Sunday Harbour Spikers had to get through to the finals first. They needed all the sideline support they could get. So Coral handed her money over to the man with the moustache. He smiled as he admired her new waistcoat. "Oh, that is fabulous on you, girl!"

Coral smiled politely and turned on her heel. The game had already started but the girls managed to squeeze into a small gap in the crowd. They had a good view of the game too. The Spikers were down by three points.

"C'mon, Spikers!" hollered Coral enthusiastically. A few more minutes passed and the Spikers managed to make up a few points, but the players still appeared to be out of sync with each other. And there was none of the usual encouraging back-slapping and high-fiving between the team members. The boys in particular appeared very straight-mouthed and stern, while the only two girls on the team seemed to hide behind nervous smiles.

The players were older than Coral and Nicks, but the girls still knew each one of them by name. Everyone at school knew the Spikers – they really were popular. Just at that moment the captain – a boy called Rory – jumped in the air and served the ball over the net. One of the Biscuit Bay Bombers jumped even higher and volleyed the ball right back at Rory. But Rory wasn't quite ready and the ball landed with a smack on his forehead and he fell to the ground.

"Augh, Rory!" cried his teammate – a boy called Jasper. "You're not meant to catch it with your head!"

Rory looked furious and embarrassed at the same time.

A Bomber quickly served and this time two Spikers both jumped for it. They collided mid-air, missed the ball entirely and scowled at each other.

"What is going on?" whispered Nicks in Coral's ear. "The Spikers are famous for their teamwork!"

But there was no time for Coral to reply. A Bomber served the ball over the net and a Spiker called Jack made a dive for it. But instead of hitting it back over the net, he hit the ball out.

"That was an easy shot!" cried his teammate, Duncan.

"Then why didn't you make it?" replied Jack, furiously dusting beach sand from his bottom.

Suddenly almost every Spiker seemed to have something angry to say, and loudly too. Coral and Nicks stared at the teammates who had been best friends not too long ago but now only seemed to growl at each other. Friendship was not something to be taken lightly, and nobody knew this better than Coral and Nicks. Best mates (and love of course) made the world turn. So where exactly had it all gone wrong?

2

the trouble with love

There may have been a small miracle involved, but somehow the Spikers managed to pull themselves together and beat the Biscuit Bay Bombers by one teensy point. There should have been cheers, hoots and hugs from the winning team, but they were strangely subdued. The two female players – Jemima and Emily – seemed happy enough, giving each other and the rest of the team congratulatory pats on the back, but the lads skulked around, pretending to search for their sports bags instead.

Coral stared and tugged her earlobe thoughtfully. What was going on? It was very frustrating. Not only was she nosy, she also didn't like to see their favourite volleyball team so down in the dumps. Just what had come between them?

"I don't like this one bit," she murmured.

"Me neither," replied Nicks. "If this continues the Spikers don't stand a chance of beating the Dune High Decoys in a few weeks' time. Sunday Harbour will lose the tournament final for sure."

The girls' shoulders slumped. The volleyball trophy had been in Sunday Harbour's trophy display cabinet for three years running. At this point it looked unlikely that it would make a fourth year. This was bad news. Not only was beach volleyball the town's favourite sport, but it was also the *only* sport they were pretty good at. The volleyball trophy had had a rather lonely time in the trophy cabinet, but the thought of the cabinet sitting entirely empty for all to see was almost too much to bear. It was even more unbearable for Nicks, who had begun assisting the editorial team on the local newspaper. She'd been helping with picture selection for the sporting section of the magazine, although it was less of a sporting section and more of a volleyball section. Nicks felt like she was practically one of the Spikers.

"Jemima and Emily might have the answer!" she announced determinedly. Coral nodded her agreement and marched alongside her friend until they found the two female volleyball players plopped down on the beach sand, kneading their weary legs.

"Hi, Jem. Hi, Em," they said in unison.

The older girls glanced up and squinted into the sun. "Oh, hi there," they said. It was clear that they recognised the younger girls, but did not know their names.

"I'm Coral and this is my best friend, Nicks."

Jem and Em nodded. And then Jem smiled. "Interesting waistcoat, Coral."

Coral glanced down at her waistcoat and looked almost surprised (she'd forgotten all about her bargain find). "Yuh, thanks," she replied quickly. "Jem and Em, is... um... everything all right with the Spikers?"

Jem and Em stared at the girls for a few moments and then shrugged and chewed on their lips unhappily.

"It's just that... well, it's obvious that something is up," said Nicks.

"We'd really like to help if we can," added Coral.

"We just cannot lose the volleyball final!" declared Nicks, who knew just as well as anyone that Sunday Harbour was a small but very proud seaside town.

Finally, Jem spoke up. "Yes, something is

definitely up. And her name is Cecily." The older girl seemed almost relieved to finally say the name out loud.

"Cecily the head cheerleader?" cried Coral and Nicks at once. *She was only the prettiest and most popular girl at their school.*

Em nodded in an *I'm-afraid-so* sort of way.

"But what has Cecily done to the Spikers?" asked Coral.

"What has she not done!" harrumphed Jem with fury in her eyes.

This didn't really answer her question so Coral turned to Em hopefully.

"That Cecily," muttered Em dismally, "has spent this entire summer holiday madly flirting with Rory, Duncan, Jack *and* Jasper, and now they aren't even talking to each other any more."

"Madly flirting?" murmured Coral and Nicks.

"Oh yes!" replied Jem with a nod. "On Friday she went to the cinema with Rory.

And on Saturday she met Duncan at the Milkshake Shack."

"The next day she was giggling with Jasper on a bench at the beach," added Em with a frown. "And every Thursday afternoon she keeps Jack company while he works at his mum's garden centre. The girl is diabolical. But the boys blame each other, not her. It's so out of order."

"They're all so in love with her," agreed Jem hopelessly. "They've always been competitive, but before it used to be *for* the team. Now they're all intent on working *against* each other."

Coral and Nicks listened to every word spoken by the two older girls before turning to face each other. It was obvious they were thinking exactly the same thing. Finally they turned back to Jem and Em.

"Cecily isn't exactly a bad sort," said Coral out loud.

Nicks also looked confused. "Yes, she's

always seemed quite careful with other people's feelings before now."

They both paused and stared up at the blue sky for a few moments. Coral was thinking about the time Cecily didn't laugh at her for walking straight into a lamppost in front of (practically) the entire school. Nicks was remembering the day that Cecily personally thanked her for selling the most raffle tickets to raise money for the new school flag.

"That may be, but she's still a troublesome flirt!" growled Jem.

"And a ferocious four-timer!" grumbled Em.

But they didn't have time to say more because suddenly there came the sound of loud laughter near them. The day was getting on and cooling quickly and the beachfront was emptying rapidly, so it was not difficult to spot who was making the noise. Coral and Nicks turned to see Duncan and Cecily sitting on a picnic bench in the shadow of a very low tree. The laugh had belonged to him. Cecily was just as amused, but hers was more of a delicate giggle. The girls watched as she brought her sparkly nails to her mouth, her eyelashes fluttering like butterfly wings. She then swung her glossy, strawberry-blonde curls over one shoulder and lifted her chin so that the soft, pale skin of her neck flashed in the fading sunlight. There was no doubt about it – the girl was in full-throttle flirting mode.

But perhaps Jem and Em were wrong. Maybe Cecily really did love Duncan. *Just* Duncan.

It was like Jem had read Coral's mind.

"Don't be fooled," she groaned. "She behaves like that with the rest of the team too."

Coral's shoulders slumped. She felt let down. She'd always liked Cecily. In fact, she had been working on being just like her one day. But as a dedicated champion of romance, she now realised that Cecily clearly had the wrong idea about love. Unless…

"Einstein moment!" she announced loudly. "Just leave it to us, we'll sort this out."

lessons in love

"It's fate!" declared an excitable Coral to Nicks as they walked double-time in the direction of Nicks's house. It would be dark soon.

"Really..." murmured Nicks with a vague nod (because it was not always wise to encourage Coral).

"Definitely! We have been personally summoned by Aphrodite the goddess of love."

"Personally, huh?" Nicks quickly sidestepped a boy on a skateboard without slowing down.

"Well, maybe not personally, but it was absolutely our destiny to witness Cecily's behaviour for ourselves. It made me realise just how desperately the poor girl needs the services of the Cupid Company. She should most definitely become our next client."

Nicks did not look convinced. "But we're matchmakers, remember? Cecily doesn't seem to have any problems finding a boyfriend, Coral."

"Matchmakers!" replied Coral indignantly. "We are far more than just matchmakers. We are Cupid's arrow. We are Aphrodite's co-workers. We are love's sat nav. And it's all suddenly very clear to me. Only this time our mission is quite different. This time we have to help Cecily, er... *love a little less*."

"Mmm. So instead of helping her find romance, you mean we help her to find *less* romance?" replied Nicks, looking confused.

"Exactly," said Coral. "We have to point Cecily in the right direction and help her to find true love. Right now she is simply lovestruck with four boys at once. It would be much better for the Spikers if she gave up on all of them altogether and found someone completely new."

Nicks gave this some more thought. It would certainly be a different direction to the one they were used to. But there was the volleyball team to think about. By helping Cecily they would put the Spikers back on track and unite the team to victory.

"Coral – this time you have definitely experienced an Einstein moment!" declared Nicks finally. She then put her head down and starting thinking through ideas to jot down. *This really would be a different sort of challenge. Just how would they get Cecily to focus her affections?*

"Hello, Romeo!" Coral called out. They had arrived at Nicks's house to find the caramel and white terrier pup waiting on the top step of the porch. The Westie dog, Miss Honey, was not far away. The two pups were still hopelessly in love.

Coral knelt down and fussed over her pet. She scratched his head, tickled his chin and gave him a squeeze. Truth be told, she'd missed him today. They used to go everywhere together, but now Romeo often hung back and canoodled with Miss Honey instead. Of course Coral was pleased he'd found love. After all, wasn't that what life was really all about? Still, it had taken some getting used to, though it helped that Miss Honey belonged to Nicks's mum's boyfriend, Ben, so Coral always knew where Romeo was.

"Hi, Ben!" said Nicks just a little too loudly. She had a really wide grin on her face that looked completely forced. Coral recognised the signs. Nicks's mum and Ben hadn't been dating all that long and Nicks wasn't sure about him. Coral liked him though. He was the manager at the aquarium and had all sorts of interesting things to say.

"So Ben, how is that blowfish getting on?" Coral asked now.

Ben chuckled and his kind eyes crinkled up at the corners. "Still shooting straight to the top of the tank every time it gets a fright!" he replied.

"Scaredy fish!" Coral and Ben both laughed together loudly. Nicks tried to join in but made more of an uneasy *chug-chug* sort of sound.

"Hello, girls." Nicks's mum stepped through the screen door of the house and on to the porch. Miss Honey sat up straight and wagged her tail instantly. Soft and round, she was a girly sort of girl dog who loved Ben very much but clearly enjoyed having another female around too. She especially loved the new pink bow in her fringe and the sparkly-studded collar around her neck.

Nicks's mum stared at Coral's shiny waistcoat for a moment and then smiled. "That's a rather distinctive-looking waistcoat," she commented.

Coral glanced down at her new fashion item and then turned back to Nicks's mum with narrowed eyes. Was that a compliment? she wondered.

"I just mean that I haven't seen one quite like it before," added Nicks's mum.

"That's because it's a theatre masterpiece – a work of art," explained Coral.

"We bought it second-hand from the theatre company's stall at the seaside market," added Nicks matter-of-factly.

"This waistcoat has seen its share of the bright lights – it's *vintage*," added Coral whose face said *'SECOND-HAND, PAH!'*).

"It's eye-catching and quite unusual," said Ben with an interested nod.

"It certainly is," agreed Coral. "And look, it even has a pocket." She rubbed her fingers against its satin lining. This waistcoat was useful as well as eye-catching. "Ooh, hold on, this pocket isn't empty," she suddenly murmured.

"I hope you haven't found a used tissue," yelped Nicks with a wrinkled-up nose. Miss Honey wrinkled her nose up too, as if she understood everything.

"There's more than one thing, there's..." added Coral in a breathy voice, "a piece of paper and a coin." She held both up in the air and then brought them close to her nose for inspection. The coin was copper with a star on one side and the words ONE PENNY pressed into the other. It didn't look familiar. Next she unfolded the paper, square by square. "It's got writing across it," she whispered out loud.

"It's probably a shopping list," said Nicks, who was fed up with the waistcoat already and desperately wanted to get back to Cupid Company business. *They had so much to do!*

"It looks like a letter," revealed Coral. She began reading:

My dear Sam,

This letter is a difficult one to write but the time has come for me to say goodbye to you and this lovely little seaside town. I am not getting any younger and there is still so much I need to discover about myself. And it is something I need to do alone. I will miss the company and closeness we have shared for the past six years but will always keep your love and those memories alive in my heart. How I shall miss old Mr Morris Minor! Do take care of yourself and perhaps we will meet again one day – in this life or the next. Be happy always.

Yours,

CBA

For a few moments nobody spoke. Even the pups remained stock still, their furry ears stirring slightly in the cool evening breeze.

"Poor Sam," murmured Ben thoughtfully.

"What were the chances of you finding a letter like that?" commented Nicks's mum. She was a schoolteacher and quite used to giving most things careful consideration.

Nicks set her jaw and rested her chin in her hand. She sighed. When it came to Coral, the chances of finding something out of the ordinary were usually rather good. Drama and her best friend went together like salt on a sea breeze. And of course Nicks knew exactly what was coming next.

"There's only one thing for it," declared Coral. "We must track poor heartbroken Sam down and help him – or her – find love again!"

Nicks groaned. She really had hoped to make the Spikers their priority. Sunday Harbour depended on it.

love in many languages

Coral Hut always looked its brightest and most beautiful first thing in the morning. The pale-gold early sunlight shone down on the beach like a light from heaven and the hut's yellow, mint-green and pale pink painted stripes sparkled like sugar crystals in the glow.

Inside the hut, the girls sat perched on the daybed – one at each side – surrounded by cool, whitewashed walls and pretty patterned rugs and cushions. Romeo and Miss Honey lay cuddled up near the door, enjoying the beachy views.

"We really do have a lot to do," said Coral thoughtfully.

Nicks was busy making notes but paused to nod. "Yup, we have two rather complex Cupid Company cases. Now, what are we going to do about Cecily and the Spikers?"

Both girls fell silent. Nicks tapped her pen. Coral chewed her thumb. Nicks scratched her head. Coral exhaled loudly and stared through the open door at the small, curling waves crashing on the beach.

A tall, athletic young man appeared, running along the sand with a bright orange towel hanging around his neck. He stopped with his back to Coral Hut, put the orange towel on the sand and immediately waded into the ocean. And then he was gone, swimming freestyle and cutting through the waves in the direction of the horizon. He was obviously a very good swimmer and was a small speck in no time at all.

"Maybe we should concentrate on the mystery of Sam first?" Coral finally suggested.

Nicks nodded her agreement. "Let's begin by analysing the letter for clues to Sam's identity."

But Coral was one step ahead of her friend and had already got the letter open. She scanned its contents before speaking. "Mmm, so CBA used to live in Sunday Harbour but has now moved far away."

Nicks stared at her detective friend. She had clearly been hoping for more than that.

"But is CBA a man or a woman?" she asked. "Because Sam could be a woman or a man too."

"Oh, CBA is definitely a woman," announced Coral with conviction as she held the letter up to Nicks. "See, patterned paper. And look at the writing – it's pretty and wavy. Also, 'discovering yourself' is more of a female thing to do. And as for keeping 'those memories alive in my heart' – that's a woman's touch too."

Coral hadn't proved a thing, but what she was saying did make sense.

"I agree," replied Nicks. "CBA is probably a woman. And I think she – and Sam – are both older because only old people talk about 'not getting any younger'. And young people don't think about meeting in the next life; they're too busy with this one. As for 'Mr Morris Minor', CBA clearly states that he's old too. Old people have old friends."

Coral considered this for a silent moment and bobbed her head up and down. And then her face crumpled. "So Sam is a lonely old man," she whispered. "How sad."

But Nicks was still focused on the facts. "We're really not much closer to finding out *who* Sam is though."

"Maybe the coin—" began Coral. And then

she stopped. She'd just been blinded by a giant roll of aluminium foil walking right past the hut. Nicks had seen it too. Both girls jumped up and tiptoed across the floor as if it was made of hot coals. Stopping at the door, they stared for a few silent moments.

It wasn't a walking roll of aluminium foil but a small woman wearing a shiny, silver-quilted tracksuit. She looked older than their parents but younger than their grandparents, and her skin was tanned with deep wrinkles that looked like cracks in the mud at the bottom of a dried-up river.

The silver and brown woman hadn't noticed the girls. Quietly, she climbed the stairs and unlocked the door to the neighbouring red beach hut which had recently acquired a plywood FOR RENT sign. The hut had been sitting empty ever since their previous neighbours, Malcolm and Meredith, had left for their honeymoon.

Suddenly Romeo gave a short, sharp bark.

He'd also noticed their new neighbour. The silver and brown woman heard the bark and quickly glanced over at Coral Hut, while Miss Honey simpered at Romeo as if he was the bravest dog in the world.

"Howdy, neighbours!" the woman cried out, waving.

Coral and Nicks were still mesmerised.

"Hiya," they finally managed in reply.

"Gorgeous day, darlings!" she added as she yanked the FOR RENT sign from the deck post and snapped it in half over her knee.

"Yes, gorgeous..." they echoed.

"Give me five minutes – let me get settled," added the woman, "and then why don't you mosey on over for a pot of herbal, alrighty?" She flashed them a grin, her white teeth appearing luminous next to her suntan. Her cropped hair was also white, although it was difficult to tell if it was naturally white or bleached that way.

"Uh yeah... sure..." mumbled the girls

together, even though they had no idea what a pot of herbal might be. But they waited the required five minutes – their Cupid Company business entirely forgotten – before 'moseying' on over.

The red beach hut was definitely changed since they had last visited Malcolm and Meredith there. Now the walls were covered in canvas squares of art in very bright colours. There was an easel in one corner and a long, narrow table in the other. The table was cluttered with tubes of paint, jars of brushes, a sketching pad, a couple of oil lamps, a small gas stove with a battered metal teapot and a basket of mismatched canisters and containers. The artworks were all paintings of animals of every kind – from an albatross to a zebra and almost every beast in between.

"Do you like them?" asked the woman as she stared up at the paintings lovingly.

The girls were surprised by the question.

"Oh yes!" replied Coral.

"We love animals, definitely."

"We even have a dog called Romeo. Well, two dogs—"

But the woman interrupted Coral with another question. "Kumquat or acai?"

Coral looked confused for a moment. "Er, Romeo is a Jack Russell Terrier actually."

The woman giggled at this. "No, silly. I mean would you like kumquat or acai tea. I make my own exotic herbal and fruit teas."

The girls shrugged. They'd never tried a kumquat or an acai-thingie so it really made no difference.

"I'm Zephyr, by the way," said the woman, who now had her nose buried in one of the canisters from the basket.

The girls stared silently, and practised mouthing her strange-sounding name – *Zef-er... Zef-er...*

The woman glanced up. "Zephyr!" she said again. "I chose it myself. It means a light, gentle wind. And that's exactly what I am: a light, gentle wind floating around the world. Now, what are your names?"

It took Coral exactly two and a half seconds to fall in love with the notion of an exotic-sounding name of her own. Suddenly the name Coral sounded very dull and uninteresting by comparison. And of course it said nothing about the girl herself. Very quickly her mind went to work considering all the various options...

"I'm Nicks," replied Nicks in the meantime. She waited a moment for Coral to introduce herself, but her friend seemed to be staring into the distance with glazed eyes. So Nicks filled in the silence. "And this is my best friend Coral."

Coral suddenly lurched upright and grinned. "Call me Amor!"

Zephyr seemed to like this. "Amor – meaning 'love' in many languages. Oh, how simply divine!"

Coral, or Amor, grinned. Of course she

knew what it meant – love was her specialist subject, after all. And as a true champion of love, it really was the perfect name.

Nicks's nose wrinkled as she contemplated Amor, the girl who meant 'love' in many languages. It wasn't that she disliked the name, because – just like her best friend – she also loved 'love' very much. In fact, it really was top of her list of favourite things in the world. But Coral's name was Coral, not Amor. And if everyone just went about changing their name when the mood took them, well – the world would be a chaotic place (and Nicks was more of an ordered sort of girl).

She continued to watch her friend, who was now very busy telling Zephyr all about the Cupid Company and the work they did for love. She also listened as her friend slotted her new name into her chit-chat at every available opportunity. Coral, now-known-as Amor, also seemed to have developed a sudden

fancy for words like 'darling' and 'divine'.
Nicks breathed deep and narrowed her gaze.
Just when they really had so many other
things to concentrate on...

on the case

Zephyr was just like her name. She really did float around the world. She had already lived in more than thirty different places and still planned to live in quite a few more, if she could. She sold her art to pay for the things she needed. Animals were her favourite subject to paint, and they were her favourite subject to talk about too.

Romeo and Miss Honey had joined them at

the red beach hut and already seemed right at home with Zephyr, who was stroking their fur with her bare toes while sipping kumquat tea and sharing stories of her life. She'd been to the Brazilian rainforests to see the red-eyed tree frog. She'd travelled all the way to the desert for the spotted hyena. She'd even visited the plains of Africa to glimpse the Big Five (and had seen at least one elephant, rhino, lion, buffalo and leopard). Animals really *were* her thing.

"So what brings you to Sunday Harbour?" wondered Nicks out loud.

Zephyr exhaled, making a sound like a light wind. "When you reach my age you find yourself tiring quicker." She sighed again. "I've spent most of my life travelling and seeing the animals, but it's starting to prove a rather solitary existence. I suppose I do get a bit lonely. Perhaps it's time to settle down somewhere and make some human friends. But I would miss the animals..."

"We have an aquarium in Sunday Harbour," offered Coral hopefully. "It's a really good one, and Nicks's stepdad is the manager too."

Nicks turned an instant crimson. "Ben is my mum's *boyfriend*!" she hissed.

Coral turned her nose up like she didn't think that was relevant. After all, Ben and Nicks's mum were clearly mad about each other. It was definitely love, so of course they'd get married one day. She turned to face their exotic and very interesting animal-loving neighbour.

"I speak for my best friend Nicks and myself – Amor – when I say that this is a darling seaside town and that it would be divine if you stayed here."

Zephyr chuckled and abandoned her mug on the table. "I don't know that I'm quite ready for that yet, girls. For now this is just a little seaside holiday. But I'd love to paint a portrait of your pups."

"That would be gorgeous!" yelled Coral excitedly.

Nicks turned to her friend with a weary look. "Yes, a portrait of the pups would be nice. And you and I have urgent Cupid Company business to see to," she hissed.

"Oh my," cooed Zephyr. "Are you on a case? Can you tell me about it?"

"We're on two cases actually," replied Nicks politely (although they'd never called it a 'case' before).

"I'd love to hear more," pleaded Zephyr.

While Nicks felt that confidentiality was key to the Cupid Company, Coral clearly couldn't wait to tell their new neighbour all about the trouble created by the flirtatious Cecily amongst the Spikers. She also ended up revealing how they hoped to help Cecily find true love, just as soon as they came up with a plan.

Zephyr listened with obvious interest. And then she froze, held her breath and spoke out loud in a hurried sort of way. "I could help you to help Cecily find her lovebird!" she cried out. "I am, after all, a bit of an animal expert, and humans are nothing more than smart, civilised animals – or some of them are at least. Did you know that, just like humans, many animal species also use impressive courtship rituals to attract a partner? Take the male bowerbird, for example – he fills his nest with bright things like shells, coins and pebbles to attract the female's attention. That's his animal bling. Animals also like to dance, make special sounds, get touchy-feely and put on displays of beauty or fighting prowess to catch the fancy of a mate."

The girls thought about this for a few moments. And then they both leaned forward, interested enough to hear more.

Zephyr leaned forward eagerly too. "It's all about helping Cecily to connect with her animal instincts. I believe that right now she's simply a confused young lady."

Nicks nodded in agreement. "Cecily really is nice enough."

Zephyr continued wisely. "You'll need to find out more about Cecily before you can help her to find her lovebird."

Coral grinned. "We're one step ahead of you. We already have a Cupid Company questionnaire which we hand out to all our new clients so that we can get to know them better."

Nicks reached for her butterfly clipboard, which just happened to have a questionnaire pinned to its front. She passed it to Zephyr, pleased that they were such an efficient, organised matchmaking company. Zephyr's eyes zigzagged across the sheet.

"Mmm, right," she murmured as she read. "It's not bad, but it needs some rewriting." She slipped the clipboard's pen from its holder and started scribbling, reading out loud as she wrote. "What is your favourite smell? What animal best describes you and why?"

Coral nodded. She was usually open to new ideas, and she thought the revised questions could be useful. But Nicks did not look convinced.

"Trust me," said Zephyr with a wink. "The prairie vole, black vulture, wolf, barn owl, condor, bald eagle, gibbon ape... these are just some of the animals that mate for life. They have a lot to teach us." Zephyr waved the revised questionnaire in the air. "Now all you have to do is ask Cecily to complete the questionnaire."

Nicks squinted into the sunlight and Coral scratched an itch.

"Yes, about that..." she murmured.

"Cecily hasn't actually signed up to the Cupid Company yet," explained Nicks.

Zephyr bit her lip thoughtfully. "So Cecily might be quite happy dating *all* the Spikers?"

"It's just the boys she wants to date," replied Coral optimistically. "And I don't think she even knows all the trouble she's causing."

Zephyr leaned back in her chair and took a long sip of kumquat tea. "There's only one thing for it, girls. We're going to have to sit that Cecily down and tell her all about the prairie voles, black vultures, wolves, barn owls, condors, bald eagles and gibbon apes."

Zephyr had said 'we', like she was a member of the Cupid Company too. Nicks's eyes narrowed. She had a sudden and very strong suspicion. Something told her that they would be getting a lot more advice from their new neighbour in the future – whether they asked for it or not.

Picture Perfect

Back at Coral Hut, Nicks flipped through a set of recent photos of the Spikers. "Coral, I think that we should ask Jem and Em for their help," said Nicks.

"Amor," replied Coral, "call me Amor."

Nicks sighed. "Why?"

"Why?" Coral looked surprised. "Well, because I just don't feel like a Coral any more."

Nicks had no idea what a Coral was

supposed to feel like and so she decided to sidestep the subject altogether. Yes, this was her strategy: she would simply avoid calling Coral (or Amor) anything at all.

"Well, erm, *my friend*, if we want Cecily to complete our questionnaire we're going to have to come up with a plan." Nicks stared dismally at the photographs. She compared them with earlier photos of the Spikers. These new photographs showed Rory, Duncan, Jasper and Jack snapping and snarling at each other. There really wasn't one she could use in the local newspaper. It simply would not do.

Coral noticed her friend's frown and leaned over to take a look at the snapshots. And then she grinned and shouted out: "Einstein moment! Those are perfect."

"Perfect for the Halloween edition of the magazine!" snapped Nicks.

"No, no, don't you see! Compare the pre-Cecily photographs of the Spikers with these latest ones and it's all the proof we need to convince Cecily to sign up to the Cupid Company. She'll soon realise that her outrageous flirting is splitting up the volleyball team. The evidence is there – in colour!"

"And as head cheerleader she's sure to have the school volleyball team's best interests at heart," added Nicks triumphantly. "You're a genius, Coral. I mean, Amor." She grabbed the questionnaire and photographs. "C'mon, I know exactly where to find Cecily."

Coral looked surprised. Nicks grinned. "It's Thursday, isn't it? Jack's mum's garden centre is just a few blocks away."

The Cupid Company (which had always included Romeo but now also included Miss Honey) stood tall and to attention. And then they marched, two by two, in the direction of *Plants R Us*.

The entrance to the nursery was built to look like a cave, with fake rocks and dense fringes of plants that climbed, dangled and curled around each other. Inside the nursery there was just as much greenery, although it was planted in plastic pots laid out on sloping shelves. There were also rows of taller trees and bushes all clumped together. And in the far corner there was an outdoor section that sold things like small water fountains, garden statues, sun catchers, birdhouses and sundials.

The Cupid Company slowed their pace and scanned the area before them. The only person about was a middle-aged woman who was more than likely Jack's mum. Still, it wasn't exactly a small nursery.

Coral began tiptoeing forward.

"Why are you walking like that?" whispered Nicks hoarsely, scanning the nursery nervously.

"For exactly the same reason that you're whispering," replied Coral. "We need to find Jack and Cecily before they find us. Then you'll have to distract Jack while I corner

Cecily, on her own. I'll need the questionnaire." Nicks passed it over. "And the evidence." Nicks handed the photographs over too. And then they continued tiptoeing... until finally they caught a glimpse of glossy, strawberry-blonde curls visible through the leaves of some potted lemon trees. A high-pitched, flirty sort of giggle confirmed the rest.

"Right," murmured Coral in a low voice, "now how are you going to distract Jack?"

Nicks's eyes grew in size. "I have no idea!"

"Sssh!" Coral checked on the curls. They hadn't moved. Suddenly Jack's mum (possibly) appeared to their left. She was walking towards them with a *can-I-help-you* look on her face.

"Birthday!" bleated Nicks suddenly. "I will ask Jack for help with a birthday gift!" She disappeared behind the row of lemon trees.

"Can I help you?" asked Jack's mum (most likely).

Coral smiled sweetly and patted Romeo's head. "Just looking, thanks."

So Jack's mum (almost certainly) went on her way. Coral whistled a few notes and then quickly peered between the lemons. Cecily hadn't moved. She was alone too. Coral knew she did not have much time. So she took a shortcut between a pair of lemon trees.

"Hi, Cecily!" she said as she emerged on the other side.

Cecily yelped with fright and landed a metre away.

Accepting that she could have made a less dramatic entrance, Coral quickly pulled a harmless sort of smile while she removed the leaves and lemon twigs from her curly hair. "I'm Co— I mean, Amor," she said with a small, friendly wave.

Cecily quickly calmed down and stared at Coral closely. "Oh, hi," she said. "I think I've seen you around."

Coral nodded. "I'm the one who walked into the lamppost."

"Oh, right. So you did."

"But I'm really pleased to have run into you Cecily because, you see, I'm here representing the Spikers... er, sort of."

Cecily glanced up, as if she was looking for Jack. And then she turned her attention back to Coral. She didn't speak; she just stared at Coral expectantly.

"As you know, the whole town is very proud of our volleyball team," stammered Coral with a sudden case of nerves. "They've always been such a strong, dedicated team... like best mates, practically."

Speaking of best mates, Coral suddenly noticed Nicks and Jack unexpectedly walking back in their direction. She made bulgy-eyeballs at Nicks, but it was too late.

"Hey, Cec," said Jack when they were within earshot, "this girl is looking for a birthday gift for her mum, but she doesn't like anything I've shown her. You could probably do a better job."

Cecily glanced from Coral to Nicks, both

girls staring at the ceiling as if they had absolutely no knowledge or interest in the other one.

"I was actually just busy with this girl, Jack. And the funny thing is, she wants to talk about the Sp—"

"Oh, don't mind me!" cried Coral, just a little louder than was probably necessary. "Er, you carry on."

Jack looked slightly anxious and then he shrugged, like he'd suddenly lost interest. "I've got to water the ferns before we can get out of here," he said to Cecily, who replied with a nod and a very sweet smile. She blew him a kiss and then he was gone.

Cecily turned to face Nicks. "Do you know what sort of gift you're after?"

"Well, I'm not really."

"Not really sure?" wondered Cecily.

"We're not really after a gift," explained Coral.

Cecily turned to face Coral. "Do you two know each other?"

"Yes, we do," replied Nicks guiltily. "Cor—um, *this girl* and I are actually best friends." Their plan had seemed like a good one in theory, but the reality of it...

And then Nicks remembered the Spikers. She thought about Sunday Harbour. She imagined their town's empty trophy cabinet. She pictured the local newspaper with nothing good to write about.

"Cecily," she said suddenly and with conviction, "these photographs of the Spikers were taken last season. Please take a closer look."

She handed the snaps over to a surprised and confused-looking Cecily, who slowly flicked through each one.

"And these photographs," Nicks continued, "were taken recently." She paused and gave Cecily a moment to glance through the latest photos while she mentally prepared the next part of her speech. But there really was no need. Cecily's face suddenly crumpled.

"It's all my fault!" she cried out.

"Yes, yes, it is," replied Coral matter-of-factly as she tenderly patted Cecily's shoulder.

Sparkly silver tears slid down Cecily's pretty pink cheeks. "I can't help myself." She snuffled. "I must admit, I do love the attention."

Coral and Nicks nodded. *So that was it, Cecily loved the attention.*

"We can help you to find something so much, much, much better than attention," revealed Coral, like she knew a very big secret.

Cecily wiped her pretty eyes and hiccupped. "What could that be?"

"LOVE!" said Coral and Nicks at once.

Nicks put a gentle arm around Cecily's shoulders. "Don't worry, the Cupid Company is here to help."

"The Cupid Company?"

"Think of us as representatives of love,"

replied Coral. And then she told Cecily all about the Cupid Company. Cecily listened closely until Coral was done. And then she tilted her head up to the heavens and smiled wistfully at the thought of finding true love. She certainly seemed attracted to the idea, like she'd watched enough romantic films to know vaguely what it was about.

"But how will I know when I've found true love?" she asked.

"Well, you won't want to date four boys at once, for starters," replied Coral.

Cecily looked interested. "And will my true love adore me?"

Nicks nodded. "That's what true love is all about."

"True love..." ooh'd Cecily. "OK, I'll sign up to your Cupid Company. But what about the Spikers?"

"No more Spikers," replied Coral.

Cecily's face fell. Then she mumbled something about doing it for the good of the town and finally accepted the Cupid Company questionnaire being offered to her.

Jack reappeared. He was heading their way.

"Do what's best for the Spikers, Cecily," Coral whispered hopefully.

Cecily glanced at Jack approaching and bit her lip nervously.

"Think about finding your one true love…" murmured Nicks.

Cecily stood tall and squared her delicate jaw. And then she opened her mouth, ready to speak before Jack could.

"I don't think I can help you out at the nursery any longer, Jack," she said resolutely. "But we can still remain friends." And then she turned on the heel of her pale pink pump and took great strides in the direction of the cave entrance with its fake rocks and dangling plants.

Jack watched her go with a confused expression. And then he turned slowly to face

Coral and Nicks, peering closely at each one of them.

Nicks hummed. Coral inspected her nails. And then both girls shrugged, did an about-turn and very quickly followed in Cecily's wake. Romeo and Miss Honey were not far behind.

chasing the dream

What with it being the back end of summer, the days were growing shorter and shorter, and they felt a little cooler too.

"I do love this time of day," said Nicks as she breathed in deeply. The last of the fishing boats had left and the early-morning air was salty and still.

Romeo and Miss Honey seemed to be enjoying the pale, gentle sunshine too. They ambled along side by side, the broadest parts of their pot bellies rubbing along gently.

Suddenly Romeo spied a seagull. It was perched on the sand, just a short distance away. His body stiffened and his ears pricked forward. Seagull chasing was his favourite pastime. Miss Honey paused and glanced from the seagull to her Romeo. She knew exactly what he was thinking. Her gaze narrowed and her throat trembled with the sounds of a soft growl. It was quite clear that she didn't approve of seagull chasing.

Romeo shivered. It was obviously taking all of his strength to resist. He turned to Miss Honey pleadingly. Her top lip pulled back, revealing the jagged edges of her white teeth. A tiny, almost imperceptible whine escaped Romeo. Could he stand firm? Miss Honey apparently had her doubts. So she gave one short but very loud bark and the seagull flapped its wings and flew away. Romeo closed his eyes and slumped, as if he was remembering all the good times he'd had chasing seagulls across the empty beach in the past.

In the distance, the same tall, athletic young man with the bright orange towel jogged along the water's edge. The girls watched him closely. The man and his orange towel were starting to become a common sight. They'd only recently seen him cycling along the promenade too. He always seemed to be doing some kind of exercise.

"My mum says he's training for the Olympics," said Nicks casually.

"The Olympics?"

"Yup, he's a triathlete – swimming, running and cycling."

Coral smiled. She liked the idea of a Sunday Harbour medal winner.

Nicks unlocked the double doors to Coral Hut and was about to push them wide open when something made her pause.

"Look here," she said as she stooped to scoop something off the floor. It was a sheet of paper. "It's from Zephyr," she murmured, and read:

"Clues that he/she wants to be your bull/ buck for life. Number one: he/she calls the next day. Two: he/she listens to what you have to say. Three: he/she introduces you to his/her pack/herd/colony. Four: he/she actually wants to meet your friends and pack/herd/colony and also remembers important dates.

Clues that you are a temporary mate. One: he/she takes phone calls in private. Two: doesn't introduce you to his/her pack/ herd/colony or friends. Three: talks about him/herself only. Four: has no interest in what you do."

Nicks glanced up at Coral, who shrugged. "What's that about?"

"I have no idea," replied Nicks (although a small part of her suspected she just might). "Anyway, we have important Cupid Company business to focus on. We've been neglecting our other case – Sam. I was thinking about the letter and realised that we've overlooked the most obvious clue – your waistcoat."

Coral thought about her lovely waistcoat for a moment. There probably was not another one like it out there. It was definitely a waistcoat you took notice of.

"If we're right and Sam really is a man," continued Nicks, "then he must be rather small. I mean, the waistcoat almost fits you."

"It fits me just fine," replied Coral.

Nicks shrugged and frowned. "So Sam is not a big man. And the waistcoat is from the Sunday Harbour Theatre Company. So he must somehow be linked to them."

"That's an excellent point, Nicks," agreed Coral, rubbing her chin thoughtfully. She was surprised she hadn't thought of it herself. "It's the perfect place to start looking for Sam. Or maybe someone there will recognise the coin."

Nicks glanced at the piece of paper their

neighbour had left. She really did seem determined to get involved in their Cupid Company business. "What are we waiting for – let's go right away," she replied hastily.

Coral turned to the pups expectantly. Romeo was nestled in a corner of the deck with his paw over his head while Miss Honey snored softly on the top step. Neither pup looked eager to move, so the girls left them for the theatre.

The Sunday Harbour Theatre was one of the town's oldest buildings, but with its bright yellow-gold domed roof it looked as if it belonged somewhere else. It was anything but ordinary, with pointy deep-set windows, an enormous arched doorway and stone steps that dipped with wear in the centre.

"Do we simply ask if they have a Sam here?" asked Nicks as they moved from the bright outside into the cool, dark interior of the theatre foyer. The walls were studded with glass cases containing black and white posters of actors and the air smelled of talcum powder. But there was no one about. The only sign of life was a faint drone of voices which seemed to be coming from behind the large, closed double doors.

"Hello?" said Coral, her eyes swivelling like ball bearings in her head, this way and that. She waited a few moments and then leaned in close to Nicks's ear. "Yup, we just say that we're looking for Sam. Come on, through those doors."

Nicks grabbed Coral's hand. "But I can hear people."

"That's the point. Come on, they're probably just rehearsing." Keeping a hold of her friend's hand, she pulled her along. She was first through the doors, and then she stopped.

"Maggie?" she gasped (because it still felt odd calling Nicks's mum Maggie, even though Maggie Waterman insisted upon it).

Nicks rear-ended her friend and tried to peer around her head. And then she saw it – her mum on stage, playing to an audience of two.

"MUM!"

Maggie Waterman turned to face the girls. "You caught me!" she cried out and then laughed.

"I er, had no idea you acted, Mum..." stammered Nicks.

"I don't. Mr Mancini over here is very kindly giving me some lessons on public speaking and helping me to project my voice, that sort of thing. The new school term is not far away and I've got to be ready for my pupils." She smiled at Mr Mancini to convey her gratitude.

"She's really not that rusty at all," added Ben, who just happened to be the second member of the audience.

"But it's been a long time since I taught a class of pupils," replied Maggie.

Both girls nodded and made silent O shapes with their lips, like it was all now very clear to them.

"How did you know we were here?" asked Nicks's mum.

"We didn't," replied Nicks. "We're on Cupid Company business. We're trying to find Sam, the waistcoat's previous owner."

Maggie and Ben both nodded. Of course they remembered the waistcoat. They hadn't forgotten about Sam and the letter either.

Suddenly Mr Mancini stood up. He was tall, dark and handsome with a very square jaw and a face that looked like it could be famous but actually wasn't at all. Not that he seemed to mind. He looked the happy sort, like he was pleased to make his mark in the world with the Sunday Harbour Theatre Company.

"Please do stay a while, girls. We could do with a few extra members of the audience," he announced like he was addressing a crowd. The ends of his words were clipped so that they sounded short and sharp.

Coral and Nicks hesitated; they really had a lot to do.

"Sit! Sit!" demanded Mr Mancini with a theatrical wave of his hand. He really did use his hands a lot. "Now Ben, babe, you climb up on that stage with Mags. There you go, up, up, that's it. Now, I want us to do some role-playing. Mags, dear, this will help to build your confidence. Ben, you will play the pupil – the cheeky chappie of the classroom. And Mags, you are to attempt to tutor the little rogue."

Ben smirked and Maggie giggled like a kid. And then they straightened their faces, trying to be serious. Ben became the pupil and Maggie the teacher. And they were doing OK, until Ben got a mischievous glint in his eye and pinched Maggie's bottom. She giggled and slapped his hand playfully. He then swept her up in his arms and swung her around and around the stage. It was quite obvious that they were in love and enjoying each other's company very much. But to twelve-year-old onlookers, it was all very, very embarrassing.

Nicks's warm red cheeks throbbed as she tried to make her head disappear into her neck. Coral slithered down in her chair and cackled into her cupped hands. *BRILLIANT!* She could hardly breathe, it was so funny. Her entire life she'd had two parents to embarrass her. With just a mum around, Nicks had always got off lightly. But no longer, it seemed...

"Let's get out of here," groaned Nicks with a quick goodbye wave. The Cupid Company had played a part in uniting Ben and her mum, but now she had to face the consequences and they would definitely take some getting used to. Coral was still tittering when they reached the foyer, so Nicks focused on the young man now standing behind the concession stand instead. This person might know Sam.

Quickly she made her way over to the man, who was wearing a black day suit and a name badge that said *Oscar*.

"We're not open yet," declared Oscar loudly, like others might be listening.

Nicks checked behind her. They were still the only other people in the theatre foyer. "That's OK – we don't want to buy anything. But maybe you can help us. We're looking for a man called Sam."

"Sam, huh?" announced Oscar, like it was a line from a movie. He picked up a glass and started polishing it with a cloth. "Don't think I know a Sam."

"He's probably an actor. And not a very tall one either," said Coral, who had finally managed to move on from the image in her head of Ben and Maggie Waterman cavorting on stage. Now she focused on Oscar. He looked vaguely familiar...

"He may be an actor," said Oscar as he checked the glass against the fluorescent overhead light, "but it doesn't mean I know him. We have lots of actors coming and going through here," he added, like this was the beating heart of Hollywood.

Coral stared closely at the young man's familiar face...

"Well, then maybe you'll recognise this coin?" pleaded Nicks hopefully, holding the coin up for inspection.

"Looks like somebody's lucky penny," he replied without hesitation.

The girls turned to each other and had a quick, silent best friend conversation.

A lucky penny?

Of course it is!

Finally it seemed like they were getting somewhere. "Are you sure you don't know Sam?" pleaded Nicks one last time.

Oscar stopped polishing. He stared at the girls with his hands resting on the shiny chrome counter. And then he spoke.

"Ladies, actors like me are rolling stones chasing the dream. We are nurslings of the sky; we pass through the pores of the ocean and shores we change, but we cannot die."

Nicks was lost. Coral wasn't even listening. "Oh, I know you!" she finally cried out at the top of her voice. "You're Oscar who also works behind the fish counter at Fargo's Fishmart!"

But Oscar did not reply. He simply hung up his cloth, turned slowly on his heel and started packing the fridge with cans.

Coral and Nicks waited a few moments. When it became clear that Oscar would say no more, they also did an about-turn and left the way they'd come. They sighed, not looking much happier than Oscar. *The theatre really would have been the simplest way to locate Sam, and now it looked as though they'd lost their best chance of information.*

team talk

The following morning, the girls arrived at Coral Hut feeling as bright and sunny as the new day. Romeo looked a little happier with life too as he trailed behind Miss Honey, who led the way.

"Cecily is officially a Cupid Company client now," recapped Nicks in her usual officious sort of way. "And she has a questionnaire too. I hope she's filled it in."

Coral rattled the lucky penny in her closed fist. "Now if only we can track down poor, lonely old Sam..."

"Yoooo hooo, girlies!"

Both girls' heads snapped up. It was their new neighbour, waving at them frantically from the deck of the hut next door. Today she was dressed in a shiny gold-quilted tracksuit with a matching gold plaited headband strapped to her forehead.

"Hiya, Zephyr!" called Coral, who looked impressed by their neighbour's bold outfit. Nicks was not so sure, but of course she waved back.

"Hi, Amor. Hi, Vicks," replied Zephyr.

"It's Nicks," said Nicks. But Zephyr didn't seem to hear her. She was already hurriedly making her way over to Coral Hut.

"You see," whispered Coral conspiratorially, "that's exactly the problem with a normal name – it's too easily forgotten."

"Yes, thanks for that, Miss Non-Amor,"

snapped Nicks, who still didn't believe it was OK just to suddenly change your name on a whim.

"So darlings, did you receive the note I slipped beneath your door yesterday?" asked Zephyr, who now stood at the bottom of Coral Hut's striped steps. Her eyes blinked rapidly as she waited eagerly for their reply. She was wearing gold false eyelashes.

"Yes," replied Nicks, "yes, we did."

"Oh, jolly-o," said Zephyr happily. "You see, I believe that the Cupid Company can offer a much broader service. It's not just about uniting lovebirds; we should offer advice and support to fledgling relationships as they spread their wings and learn to fly... away... together."

Coral and Nicks stared silently. Coral was considering the bird image. Nicks was still stuck on their neighbour's use of the word 'we' when referring to the Cupid Company. Nicks sighed.

But Zephyr did not seem to find their silence discouraging. "Give this to Cecily," she said, holding out a delicate lime-green feather. "It's from an actual lovebird."

"What's it for?" asked Coral.

"It's an animal charm; it will help her to find true love. But don't worry – no birds were harmed in the making of it." Zephyr seemed to think this was very funny and made loud hooting sounds like an owl.

"Would you look there!" Nicks suddenly called out, pointing in the direction of the shoreline. "The Spikers are having a practice session. Come on, Coral."

"You mean Amor."

"Come on, *chum*, I think we should see how they're getting on. Thanks for your advice, Zephyr – we shall certainly take it under advisement." She then swept down the stairs, hoping that her friend would soon follow.

"Those are some eyelashes!" commented Coral when she caught up with Nicks. But her friend was already focused on something else. She was staring at the Spikers with a narrowed gaze. Something was not right.

"Would you try catching the ball!" yelled Jasper at Jack, who had just landed belly-first on the ground, without the ball.

"I don't see you racking up any points!" cried Jack through a mouthful of beach sand.

"Maybe both of you should take up netball instead," snapped Duncan.

The girls stopped. They stared. And then they turned to each other and had a silent, best friend conversation.

What...? The Spikers seem angrier than ever!

Where has it all gone wrong?

But... but surely now that Cecily is out of the picture...?

You'd think!

Suddenly Jem and Em were on top of them. "I thought you girls said you were going to sort this out?" growled Jem.

"Yes, 'just leave it to us', you promised," added Em. "But you just seem to have made things worse!"

The girls stared, perplexed. And then Coral's spine straightened. Her head tilted left then right. And then she understood.

"The problem with boys," she said directly to Jem and Em, "is they don't communicate. They don't share their feelings like girls. And the problem we have here," she continued expertly, like a true colleague of Cupid, "is that the lads don't know that they've *all* been dumped by Cecily."

"Ohhh," replied Jem, Em and Nicks at once, like it all suddenly made sense.

Coral nodded importantly. "Jem and Em, you need to call a group meeting. And no one is allowed to leave until everyone has opened up. Got it?"

Jem and Em stood firm with their shoulders squared. "Check!" they declared with a stern nod. They then turned and marched determinedly over to the rest of the Spikers.

"I think we can leave it up to those girls," said Coral with satisfaction.

Further along the beach the lifesavers were having their own practice session. They competed in sprinting races across the hard sand at the water's edge. They launched red canoes into the water while senior lifeguards blew into whistles around their necks. They even practised sea rescues and did sit-ups and star jumps to keep fit.

The girls glanced from the lifesavers to the volleyball team. Jem and Em had corralled the lads into a circle where they now all sat with their knees touching. Jem prodded Jack, who started speaking. His chin touching his chest, he stared at the sand until he was done. Jasper spoke next, followed by Duncan. Rory the captain gave their backs a firm, friendly pat before he said his piece. Finally there were friendly pats all round.

Nicks grinned. It looked like the Spikers were back on track.

And then they saw her.

Their newest Cupid Company client had just arrived at the beach wearing a red and white polka-dot bikini. She hovered at the edge of the lifesavers' training ground, smiling sweetly and offering them small, friendly waves every so often. Nicks's grin slipped at the edges.

Suddenly Cecily performed a playful star jump. Her strawberry blonde curls sailed on the breeze. She squealed and attempted another star jump, this time leaping even higher. She was clearly trying to win the lifesavers' attention, although she soon tired of the star jumps. She stopped and giggled and pointed to her leg like she had cramp. One of the lifesavers – a tall, tanned lad – quickly stooped to massage her calf muscle. She blew him a kiss and then skipped over to one of the senior lifeguards. She touched his arm and blew into his whistle, seeming to find the shrill sound it made very funny indeed.

"I had no idea Cecily was quite so friendly with the lifesavers," considered Nicks.

"What is she doing?" murmured Coral, mesmerised. The girls weren't the only ones who had noticed her. The Spikers were watching too, but they seemed less concerned. They jumped to their feet, gave a team high-five and resumed their practice session, only this time they seemed to serve and pass better than ever. It was almost as if they were trying to prove something.

"What happened to finding her one true love?" groaned Nicks. "Didn't Cecily hear anything we said to her?"

"There's only one way to find out," replied Coral. "We'll have to ask her."

It only took the girls a few moments to reach the lifesavers, but it took them considerably longer to attract Cecily's attention. She seemed far too interested in the mouth-to-mouth lifesaving demonstration.

"CECILY!" hissed Coral like a punctured tyre.

The head of strawberry curls spun around. She saw the girls and looked guilty.

"What happened to finding your one true love?" asked Coral when Cecily drew level with them.

"I'm, er... doing research," she stammered.

"Leave the research to the Cupid Company," urged Nicks. "That's our job. You just have to complete the questionnaire."

"What, like now?"

Both girls replied with *I'm-afraid-so* nods.

"But the lifesaver boys are so... well, lovely!" She glanced over at the lifesavers. Most of them were still watching her. She giggled and waved. They waved back, wide grins frozen to their handsome faces.

"Yes, that's probably true," replied Nicks kindly (although she did not know them personally).

"And I'm quite sure they like me too," added Cecily happily.

"That's probably true as well," replied Coral gruffly. "But you can't love all of them, Cecily. It just doesn't work like that. As your agents of love you're going to have to trust us on this."

Cecily did not look convinced, but she nodded sadly anyway. "I'll just go and complete my questionnaire then," she said.

The girls gave her warm hugs to show that she really was doing the right thing and then gently directed her away from the lifesavers. That's when they noticed Coral's mum, striding purposefully down the beach in their direction. She looked her usual busy self too, with a pen stuck behind both ears. Her hair was a messy pile on top of her head. And her hands were full with lots of pieces of paper.

"Oh, girls," she cried, "there you are. I need your help, please."

"What are you organising this time, Mum?" asked Coral, who was quite used to her mum's various causes and projects.

"Don't tell me you've forgotten already."

Lunchtime? wondered Coral hopefully.

"The *Farewell to Summer Beach Party*," replied Coral's mum excitedly. "It's only a few weeks away! I know we do it every year, but there still seems to be so much to organise and arrange. And I thought that this year we could build a sand *lady*. What's your verdict?"

The girls gave it some thought. Every year the folks of Sunday Harbour built a giant sand man at the party, but a sand *lady* would be just as good.

"She could have twigs for eyelashes," Coral replied excitedly. "And a pretty hat! What about some beads? She's got to have beach accessories – like a colourful trailing scarf."

"I'm so glad you like the idea," replied

Coral's mum. "Now, could you two please help me to distribute these party leaflets?"

A party was one of the girls' favourite things in the world, ranking just one position below love. They nodded enthusiastically, although Coral's head was bobbing up and down a little more frantically. *The Farewell to Summer Beach Party really would be the perfect place to showcase her new waistcoat.* She stared at the horizon wistfully. That's when she noticed the tall, athletic young man again. Actually, she recognised his bright orange towel first. He emerged from the waves, removed his swimmer's goggles and dried himself off. Running, cycling and swimming – Mr Olympics certainly was dedicated.

on target

Nicks was the first to arrive at Coral Hut the following day. She had carefully planned it that way. They were no closer to finding Sam and she needed some quiet time to study the letter from CBA again – there had to be more clues in the writing. There was also something special about being inside Coral Hut early in the morning, all on your own. She could hear the ocean hissing and bubbling as the climbing sun warmed it. Hungry seagulls caw-cawed as they scavenged for breakfast. And the wind whooshed across a still-empty beach.

"Augh! Drat!"

Nicks glanced up. That couldn't have been a seagull.

Next she heard loud, grunting noises, and heavy breathing, followed by a very deep, long sigh. She stood up to get a better view from the daybed to see Coral at the door, awkwardly balancing a box while trying to keep a hold of Romeo and Miss Honey's dog leads at the same time.

"Could you give me a hand!" she hollered when she spied Nicks.

Nicks made a tut-tut sound and abandoned the letter to Sam on the daybed. "Why have you got the pups on their leads in the first place?" Usually they'd have the run of the beach.

Coral sighed once again. "They're not

talking," she replied, nodding at the pups. "And they refuse to walk next to each other. So I had to put them on their leads."

Nicks did wonder for a moment how Coral knew that the pups weren't talking, but she was more interested in the box her friend was carrying. "What's that?" she asked instead, reaching over.

Coral grinned. "Inside that box is a Zephyr-inspired brainwave!"

Nicks turned slightly pale.

"Go on, take a look!"

So Nicks did. Mentally, she took an inventory as she pulled each new item out of the box. "Some DVDs..." she began, "including *Love Always*, *Road to Romance*, *Cupid's Tale*, *Kiss and Tell* and *I Heart You Forever*. And one book called *Romeo and Juliet*."

"It is the greatest love story ever," replied Coral, like she'd actually read the entire book (and hadn't resorted to watching the movie instead).

But Nicks was too interested in the rest of the box's contents. One after the other she pulled out a selection of decorative padded fabric hearts and swirling foil conversation hearts with printed writing that said FOR EVER, BE MINE and LOVE BUG. There were also dangling cupids, foil garlands of red and silver hearts and a banner that said I LOVE YOU. There was even a tub of one hundred fake rose petals.

"You've dismantled your bedroom, haven't you?" she said.

Coral nodded. "Just temporarily. I'm lending it all to Cecily. If she's going to fall in love then she's got to start thinking love, love, love. And personally I find being surrounded by hearts very inspiring."

"And what about this rose oil?" asked Nicks, reading from the label of a small vial of pale liquid.

"The rose is love's flower," explained Coral like this was an absolute fact of nature.

95

"Cecily must put a drop of the oil on her pillow every night and absorb its power while she dreams. That way she'll imagine her one true love."

Nicks made a 'mmm' sound. "So this has all been inspired by Zephyr's lovebird feather, right?"

Coral gave a satisfied grin. "Exaaaactly!"

If Aphrodite the goddess of love was gazing down on anybody it was Coral, because at that very moment Cecily appeared unexpectedly at the top of Coral Hut's stripy steps.

"Top timing!" cried Coral. She couldn't wait to show their newest client her box of tricks.

But Cecily did not look quite so pleased. "I'm afraid I still haven't answered this thing," she said, waving the questionnaire dismally in the air. "I'm just no good at putting my thoughts into writing."

Nicks stared at the empty lines of the questionnaire. And even though she really didn't think it could be very difficult to fill in a questionnaire, she still put her arm around Cecily and gently steered her in the direction of the daybed. "We'll go through it together," she suggested kindly.

Cecily seemed to brighten at this. She even took a moment to admire the pale and pretty interior of Coral Hut, absorbing the gingham check and floral prints.

"It's just lovely," she cooed.

But Coral and Nicks were all business.

"Now," began Nicks, reading from the questionnaire with her pen poised, "how long have you been single for? Erm, we know the answer to that one. Next question: Describe yourself in five sentences."

Cecily stared down at the scrambling primroses before answering. "I've got blonde hair. It's curly. And my eyes are the colour of brown topaz. I'm quite tall—"

That's where Nicks stopped her. "Erm, thanks Cecily, but we know what you look like.

How would you describe... the uh, person on the inside?"

Cecily looked surprised but gave it some thought. "Well, I'm kind. I'm patient. I like to laugh. I'm quite easy-going. I never argue."

Nicks nodded as she scribbled. "And what's your worst fault?"

"Once I left the back door open and a dog ate the birthday cake my mum had left out to cool. It was for my brother. They were both pretty annoyed with me. I know it was my fault, but I said sorry twice."

"I actually mean your biggest flaw as a person."

Cecily giggled. "Oh, I see. Well, this finger," she explained, holding a forefinger in the air, "is a bit skew."

"Um, on the inside?"

Cecily frowned. She seemed to prefer talking about her outside. "Uh, I'm easily distracted?" she suggested like it was all she could come up with.

The next few questions had been written by Zephyr. "Now, what animal best describes you?"

Cecily looked put out. "I'm not like an animal at all."

"You could be a warm, furry kitten?" suggested Coral from the sidelines.

Cecily seemed to like this idea. She nodded.

"What's your favourite smell?" asked Nicks next.

Cecily looked mildly irritated. "How will this help me to find my one true love?"

"Love is primal, Cec," replied Coral. "It's about finding your soul mate. It's a primitive thing. You must get in touch with your basic instincts. Now, what is your favourite smell, please?"

"JLo's *Glow*?" replied Cecily hopefully.

Neither Coral nor Nicks had any idea what the significance of this might be, but Nicks pressed on with warming cheeks. "And er, uh, do you travel alone or in a pack?"

Cecily looked confused. "I usually just use my bicycle."

Nicks paused and chewed on her pen for a bit. "How about we move on to the next section of the questionnaire? Right, now let's find out what you look for in the perfect partner. Do you like tall or short boys?"

"Oh yes!"

Nicks paused and then ticked both boxes.

"How about Mr Smooth or Mr Rough-'n'-Ready?"

Cecily nodded excitedly. Nicks made two ticks.

"Would you prefer the sporty type or a deep-thinking intellectual?"

Cecily's grin widened. "Such great qualities!"

Tick. Tick.

"Someone outspoken or the quiet type?

"Absolutely!"

Nicks paused. Stared. And then continued. "Mr Romantic or a man's man?"

"Oh, if only there were more of them!" sang

Cecily happily. She had grown much louder too.

Nicks sighed and glanced up at Cecily pleadingly. "We're narrowing these choices down, remember?"

"I know, isn't it fantastic!" Cecily's grin almost touched her dangly earrings. She did seem to enjoy talking about boys.

So Nicks made two more ticks and continued. "OK, how about: Mr Big Shot or a fun-loving, good-time guy?"

"I JUST LOVE THEM ALL!" cried Cecily with her eyes squeezed tightly shut and her arms spread wide, like she was shouting it to the world.

Coral and Nicks stared silently. *Yes, that was the problem with Cecily: she just loved all the boys.*

Coral was the first to stand up. Squaring her shoulders, she faced their client.

"Now, Cecily," she said sternly, "calm down and breathe deep. That's it. Count with me:

one, two, three. You must understand that what makes true love special is that it's between two people."

"So I can have two boyfriends, Amor?" she asked with renewed interest.

Nicks rolled her eyes while Coral shook her head slowly. "No, Cecily, *you* are the second person. True love means you and someone else. We just have to find the right boy." She glanced down at the questionnaire Nicks had filled in. "Think hard. What's your very favourite thing about a boy, *like ever?*"

Cecily made a thinking-hard face. She nibbled her lip and blinked her eyes rapidly. "I suppose I really do love sporty boys," she finally replied.

"You love *a* sporty boy," Coral corrected her. "One. Or you will do, when we find him. That's a great help."

Nicks nodded, like it all made sense. *The volleyball team... and lifesavers...*

Coral reached for the box of love tricks.

And then she paused and thought a bit. Would all the love-stuff help Cecily to focus? It could backfire and they might just end up right back at square one. She shook her head to clear it.

"You should take this box home, Cecily," she said calmly and clearly. "Read the book. Watch the DVDs. Surround yourself with hearts and think about finding true love."

But Cecily looked distracted. Her attention had been diverted by the letter to Sam sitting open on the daybed and she reached over and picked it up.

"Poor Sam," she murmured when she had finished reading it. "You know, I once had a boyfriend who had a Morris Minor."

"You know Mr Minor!" exclaimed Nicks at exactly the same moment that Coral cried: "You know old Morris?"

Cecily's face puckered. "A Morris Minor is a car, not a Mr. It's a vintage car to be exact. The lovely Matt – he was special – used to build miniature model vintage cars. And the Morris Minor was his favourite."

"Top information!" replied Coral while Nicks clapped twice. But Cecily was too busy reminiscing about the lovely Matt to wonder why this should make the girls so happy.

Coral and Nicks turned to face each other. Now all they had to do was find the right sporty boy and one pensioner called Sam who owned a vintage car. For two optimistic twelve-year-olds this couldn't be too difficult, surely?

reverse psychology

Coral arrived at Nicks's house the following day just in time for lunch. This was no coincidence; Nicks's mum was known to make outrageous and very delicious sandwiches (Coral was particularly hoping for a round of peanut butter, blueberry jelly and bacon on wholewheat).

Romeo seemed pleased to be at Nicks's house too, and he pressed his black button nose into the crack of the front door until it was finally opened by Nicks. Miss Honey's head poked through her knees. Romeo took a step forward and sniffed the pup. Then he gave her a big lick. Miss Honey responded with a bark and a lick of her own.

"It looks like the pups have made up," commented Nicks as she stood aside to let them in.

Coral nodded absent-mindedly; she was thinking mostly about poor, lonely old Sam (and a bit about lunch too). "We really must find out what a Morris Minor looks like... after lunch," she suggested.

"We're all ready to go now," replied Nicks as she led the way into the living room, where the laptop stood open on the coffee table.

Nicks's mum was bustling about in the kitchen, so Coral stuck her head in on the way past. But the word 'hello' jammed in the back of her throat. Ben was also in the kitchen and whispering something secretively into

Nicks's mum's ear. It looked like they'd forgotten that the rest of the world existed. Coral did understand. As an agent of love she accepted that romance, especially in the early stages, could be all-consuming. So she quickly closed her mouth and continued on to the living room while Romeo and Miss Honey settled themselves into a cosy corner.

"If we know what a Morris Minor looks like maybe we'll recognise the car," said Nicks, who was oblivious to the secret kitchen whispering. "Perhaps we've already seen it driving around Sunday Harbour a hundred times before but we just didn't know that it was a Morris Minor."

Coral shrugged. "Sunday Harbour isn't that big." But it wasn't that small either.

Nicks opened the internet and typed MORRIS MINOR into the search box. There were 1,320,000 search results for the vintage car, many with pictures too. The girls stared at photographs of the cars, some with varnished wooden panelling and others with white-walled tyres. But the one thing every Morris Minor had in common were rounded wheel mouldings on the side, raised bonnets in the front and rear boots that sloped to the ground.

"So that's a Morris Minor," murmured Nicks without much enthusiasm. It was quite obvious that, just like Coral, she had never seen a car like this in real life. The girls stared dully.

"Who's hungry?" asked Nicks's mum as she walked by carrying a plate of food. "We've got peanut butter, blueberry jelly and bacon sandwiches."

Coral stood up and punched the air with the hiss of the word "YES!" on her lips. She walked down the hall to find the adults in the dining room, where Ben's arm was now draped across Nicks's mum's shoulders. She focused on the food instead. Nicks soon followed, but seemed in a great hurry to leave again. Claiming a sandwich, she marched straight back out to the living room. Ben and Nicks's mum smiled at Coral so Coral smiled back. "I don't suppose you've seen a Morris Minor driving around Sunday Harbour, have you?" she asked before taking a bite.

Nicks's mum contemplated the ceiling while she chewed. "Nope, I don't think I have," she eventually said.

"I do love vintage cars," added Ben through a mouthful of peanut butter and bacon. "Don't see many of them in Sunday Harbour though."

Coral's shoulders sagged. Sam and his Morris Minor were proving to be rather elusive.

Nicks reappeared at the dining table. She was about to claim another sandwich when her mum quickly covered her hand with her own and looked excited. "Girls, do you remember a boy called Tom Lancaster who used to attend your school?" she asked.

"Didn't he become an actor or something?" asked Coral.

"Yup. Mr Mancini told me that he's just signed up to do a film! Isn't that exciting?"

Coral nodded eagerly. "Ooooh, so we can say that we went to school with Tom Lancaster."

"He's changed his name to Tamaran Lancaster, actually. But it's the same boy."

Nicks frowned and replied before Coral could. "I just don't see the point in changing your name," she grumbled.

Nicks's mum smiled blissfully and wrapped her arms around Ben. "Sometimes women change their name for very good reason," she said with a twinkle in her eye.

Ben kissed the top of her head. "Yes, for very good reason indeed," he agreed with a happy smile.

"C'mon, Coral, let's head for the beach," mumbled Nicks, who looked distinctly uncomfortable. There was no time for Coral to protest so she grabbed another sandwich and quickly followed her friend out of the door.

Nicks was already halfway down the path, walking with her hands shoved deep in her pockets. She still had the frown etched on her forehead.

"Aren't you happy that your mum is in love?" asked Coral.

"Course I am," replied Nicks. "Love rocks. But all that kissy-cuddly stuff grosses me out. I mean, they're... like, OLD!"

Coral shrugged. "We are love's army. You should not be put off by signs of affection."

"So you'd be OK if your parents pinched each other's bottoms and did all that smoochy stuff when you're in the room?"

Coral thought about this. She really could not imagine her serious father doing anything of the sort. But there wasn't much her loopy mum wouldn't do. Coral was momentarily blinded by some mental images of her own.

"Yes, it is a bit gross," she finally agreed once she'd managed to shake her head clear. "You think they'd know better!"

"That's interesting news about Tom Lancaster though, isn't it?" said Nicks.

"I know – genius! Tamaran is far more memorable though. If we ever meet him again I'll have to mention how I've changed my name too."

Nicks harrumphed. "It's not like you've ever really met him before though, is it?"

Coral grinned wider than a Cheshire cat. "No. But it'll make a great story, won't it?!"

A beam of sunlight broke through Nicks's cloud. She grinned back at her best friend as they reached the promenade. Coral always could make her laugh no matter what.

Ahead of them, the promenade was bustling with people still eager to make the most of the brilliant sunshine. A line of rollerbladers steamed past, all following a boy who carried a singing iPod in front of him like the Pied Piper. To the left, a woman wearing tie-dye was selling beads to interested bypassers. And then Coral saw him – an old man sitting on a bench, sharing a sandwich with a seagull. His shoulders stooped and his eyes hid behind sagging, puffy lids. His clothes were mismatched and his grey hair was dishevelled, but most of all – he was all on his own.

She didn't even think about it. She was suddenly standing in front of the old man.

"Are you Sam?" she pleaded.

The old man glanced up at her and smiled. He didn't look quite as lonely when he smiled.

"No dear, the name is Herb."

"Oh."

At that moment an old woman came to sit on the bench. She cosied up to Herb and chuckled: "You're not boring the poor girl with your wartime stories, are you, Herby?"

The old man smiled again. "Nope," he replied, "just a simple case of mistaken identities."

So this wasn't Sam. Still, it had been worth a try. All around people nattered, licked ice creams, pointed at seagulls circling and searching for lunch, admired the views and simply enjoyed the last of the summer. This reminded Coral; they really did not have much time. The Cupid Company had two very important cases on the go. And they weren't getting anywhere fast with either of them.

"I still don't know how we'll find Sam," she murmured to Nicks. "And as for Cecily…"

"Look there," said Nicks, "it's Sunday Harbour's top triathlete – still going for gold."

Nicks followed her friend's pointed finger. Mr Olympics was running across the beach with his bright orange towel around his neck. They'd got to know his training routine well; no doubt he would finish his run off with a swim. "I don't think I've ever seen such dedication," added Nicks. "It's like nothing else matters to him."

"He certainly is very focused," agreed Coral.

"Now there's one boy who wouldn't chase after Cecily," joked Nicks.

Coral slowed. Her eyes glazed over with a faraway look. "THAT'S IT!" she cried out.

"What is?"

"I think you'd better call me Genius instead of Amor," said Coral with a smirk. She stepped right up close to her friend so that their noses practically touched. "All the boys love Cecily, right?"

Nicks nodded – and almost headbutted Coral.

"And that's our problem. Cecily loves the attention she gets from all the boys, which means she can't focus on any one boy in particular. Cecily needs a challenge. Cecily needs someone who doesn't fancy her at all."

"So you think we should matchmake our client who already has too many boyfriends instead of none at all,with a boy who really is not interested in her – or anything else besides training for the Olympics?"

Coral chuckled. "Cecily did say she liked the sporty sort."

"But how do we know if Mr Olympics is right for Cecily?"

"You heard it for yourself – Cecily has no type when it comes to boys. She loves all types. We can't really go wrong."

Nicks grinned. "It probably would do Cecily the world of good not to be adored for once. But, of course, if she is right for Mr O then she'll change his ways and it'll be a love match. So it really is a top plan."

"Thanks," said Coral.

"Actually, I don't think you can take full credit for this," replied Nicks. But Coral had already started walking in the direction of Coral Hut. Nicks ran a few steps to catch her up. "I am the one who said that Mr Olympics was the one boy who would not chase after Cecily... remember? Coral? Coral!"

three's company

Nicks gave up trying to convince her friend, who walked the remainder of the way to Coral Hut in silent smugness. Nicks had just spied Zephyr waiting for them on the deck of their striped hut. It would have been impossible to miss her. Today she was wearing a shiny metallic blue tracksuit, although this particular one was not quilted.

Nicks wondered what their neighbour would share with them today.

Zephyr waved when she saw them approaching. She had two stripes painted across her cheekbones, one blue and one red.

"Hi-ho, Amor. Hi-ho, Trix," she called out.

"It's Nicks," grumbled Nicks, although not quite loud enough to be heard.

"Hi, Zeph!" sang Amor happily (the name just made her feel *so out there*). "I like your face paint."

Zephyr smiled in the wisest sort of way. "The stripes are a tribute to the Navaho Indians – I'm a big fan," she replied. "They know nature better than anybody. Now looky here, I painted this sign for your beach hut."

She held up a mounted square of canvas that was painted with a picture of three lovebirds perched on a branch and the words:

The CUPID COMPANY
our nature is to nurture

118

Nicks stared at the canvas. "We have a slogan," she said. "It's *All for love and love for all.*"

Zephyr stared, blinking, like Nicks had just spoken another language. "Anyway," she finally continued, "just like the lovebird calls out to its mate, I thought that this sign would tell people about the Cupid Company. Now girls, shall we go inside and then you can tell me all about your most recent exploits with dear Cecily?"

The girls shared a look and had a silent best friend conversation.

She's a little meddlesome.

Coral made a sad face. *Poor Zeph, she's just lonely.*

Forget about lovebirds, she may be more cuckoo.

But we're all she has in Sunday Harbour.

Nicks sighed like she had no choice but to agree. But she would leave it up to Coral to update the shiny blue lady; Nicks wanted to concentrate on formulating a first date plan for Mr Olympics and Cecily. She had a few possible ideas spinning around her head too, but it was very difficult to think over Zephyr.

"If you're right and this Mr O is only interested in his sports," Zephyr declared loudly when Coral was done, "then it will not be easy to get him to agree to a first date."

"So what do you suggest?" asked Nicks, mostly out of kindness (she truthfully did not like to think of anybody having nobody, especially in a friendly town like Sunday Harbour).

"We've got to let Mr O think that he's won something," replied Zephyr excitedly. "Winning is most certainly what drives a lad like our Mr O. We'll say that we're from the Beach Huts Association and tell him that we're promoting the community and rewarding those locals we believe act as outstanding role models with a complimentary beach breakfast. It's a small, transparent lie – won't hurt anybody."

The girls listened closely and wondered where this would lead.

"And then," continued Zephyr with certainty, like she regularly shared a cloud with Aphrodite, "we'll arrange a nice breakfast inside your hut, with Cecily lying in wait, primped and ready to meet her king of the jungle."

Both girls frowned and looked a little lost, but Zephyr did not even notice. "Now, our first job is to locate Mr O," she said.

"That's easy," replied Coral. "We saw him running along the beach. He's probably having his swim now. He always leaves his bright orange towel in the same spot on the sand."

Zephyr clapped. "Super-duper. We'll wait for him to emerge from the waves. Then we'll pounce on him, and quickly advise him of his winning prize. After this, you girls will track

Cecily down. Follow her scent... see if she's left a trail. And then once you've found the girl, you must arrange the breakfast for tomorrow morning."

"Couldn't we just phone Cecily?" asked Nicks, who wasn't sure that it was entirely necessary to track a person down in a civilised place like Sunday Harbour.

Zephyr shrugged and looked mildly disappointed.

"What about the breakfast?" asked Coral, who was now beginning to think that it was all a very good idea.

"The way to a man's heart is through his stomach," revealed Zephyr. "So we'd better make it good." She looked at the girls expectantly.

"Oh yes, definitely," replied Coral. It wouldn't be the first time they had raided their fridges at home in the quest for love.

"Now let's go, team, it's time to find Mr Olympics!" cried Zephyr.

The trio trudged down to the shoreline, the shiny blue lady and the girl with flyaway reddish-brown hair leading the way. Coral located the splodge of orange towel on the beach and pointed it out to Zephyr. They marched straight over and immediately stood on either side of the towel, waiting for Mr O. Nicks was slower to follow. She was contemplating all the ways this gung-ho plan could go wrong.

Both Zephyr and Coral were beginning to sag by the time Mr O finally emerged from the water. Nicks, who had been sitting sensibly on the sand and writing in her notepad, glanced up. They'd never seen Mr Olympics close up. He was very handsome as well as tall and athletic. Cecily would most certainly like this boy (although this was never in much doubt).

"Stop, please!" declared Zephyr. Mr O stopped and stared at the shiny old lady with painted stripes on her face.

"We are from the Beach Huts Association," said Coral in a loud, slow voice, like it was something she had rehearsed in her head. "And you've won. Because uh, it's all about the community. You're a very good role model for the people of Sunday Harbour. So you get a complimentary beach breakfast."

Mr O nodded, like he wasn't entirely surprised he'd won a prize for something. "Thank you," he said. "Thank you very much. Do I get a breakfast hamper then?"

"Nope." Coral shook her head. "As we're from the Beach Huts Association, you get to have breakfast in that striped beach hut over there. Ooooohaaa." She pointed to Coral Hut and added the sound effect to make the prize sound extra exciting.

"When?" asked Mr O, like he had a training schedule to consider.

"Tomorrow morning?"

"Can do," replied Mr O. "Now, do you need to give me a certificate or something?"

"We'll get it to you later," replied Zephyr.

"Right, OK," said Mr O as he checked his watch. "Now, I must get going."

Coral and Zephyr grinned and waved while Mr O grabbed his towel and turned away.

"Excuse me," said Nicks in her usual officious sort of way, "but we'll need your name for the certificate."

Mr O turned back again and nodded seriously. "Of course you will. It's J.T. Brooker."

Nicks smiled politely. "Thank you, J.T. Brooker. Our representative, Cecily, will meet you at the striped beach hut tomorrow morning."

"Cecily, huh?" grunted J.T. as he committed the name to memory. "By the way, I follow a strict diet," he added as he patted his muscular belly. *Pat-pat.* "High carb, high protein, low fat, no junk." And then he was gone, jogging down the beach at a rapid pace.

They waited until he was a small speck and all cheered (even Nicks looked like she was behind the plan now). And then Coral put her arms around her new friend and her very best friend. The Cupid Company had expanded – for now, anyway.

the prize

The wicker basket was covered in a cotton cloth printed with red lips. It wasn't subtle, but it was the closest the girls could get to a romantic sort of tablecloth. Coral had also borrowed her mum's second-best plates and cutlery and Nicks had found two plastic flutes for the fruit juice. The serviettes were paper but they looked quite pretty folded like fans. And there was a basket of oatmeal muffins and croissants with real butter and strawberry jam in a miniature screw-top jar, a dish of boiled eggs, a couple of pots of yoghurt, some fresh fruit and granola bars.

Coral balanced a plastic tray of cocktail sausages in her hand. "They'll go perfectly with the eggs," she argued.

"Egg and sausage is not the same as cold boiled eggs and cocktail sausages on sticks," replied Nicks.

"They taste the same."

"They don't look the same."

They heard Zephyr arrive and while Nicks went out to greet her, Coral took the opportunity to delicately arrange the sausages on sticks with the boiled eggs.

"Hi, girls," sang Zephyr as she sailed past Nicks, straight into the beach hut. She jiggled the leopard-print cloth she had draped across her shoulders like a wrap and excitedly demanded: "So what do you think?" The girls shrugged. It was bold but not unusual for

Zephyr. Nothing she wore was tame. "It's for our lovebirds," explained Zephyr. "I shall spread it across your daybed for them to sit upon. I'm hoping it will stir their animal instincts."

With the leopard-print wrap now transported from shoulders to daybed, Zephyr's true outfit was revealed. Today she wore a black velour tracksuit with gold trim and gold leather lace-up shoes that matched her gold lipstick.

"The gold is in honour of Mr Olympics," she explained brightly. "And today, girls, the Cupid Company is going for gold! Ooh, I do like what you've done with the breakfast."

But the girls were distracted by Cecily, who had just appeared on the deck. She looked very excited and had obviously been up very early, preparing for her date. She'd styled her hair into long, loose waves and wore a sea-green skirt that clung to her hips and then tapered, rather like a mermaid's tail. Her top was strapless with scalloped edges and she carried a little bag that was shaped like a clam with a clasp.

She giggled nervously. "I've gone with an ocean theme," she explained as she smoothed her skirt. "I mean, I've never had a first date in a beach hut before!"

She looked just like a sea queen, which could have its advantages. The girls smiled nervously. They both felt a twinge of guilt. After all, they were setting poor Cecily up with a boy who wasn't interested in finding a girlfriend at all.

It's for her own good, thought Coral in silent, best friend conversation mode.

But she's gone to so much trouble getting ready.

She still takes the business of romance too lightly.

Too true.

And she'll never find true love if she doesn't take it more seriously.

"So uh, J.T. should be here soon," mumbled Nicks out loud as she checked her wristwatch.

"Yes, very soon," agreed Coral. "And don't worry – we'll be in the hut next door if you need us."

Nicks looked surprised, but there was no time to say anything. "Good luck, darling!" cried Zephyr as she exited Coral Hut.

"Erm, if your date mentions a prize or the Beach Huts Association, just nod like you know what he's talking about," advised Coral before she followed Zephyr out.

This left Nicks standing in between Cecily and the eggs and cocktail sausages on sticks. "Don't forget," she said gently, "you're here to find your one true love." And then Cecily was all alone.

But not for long. The Cupid Company – all three of them – were poised on the deck of the red hut next door. "He's coming!" rasped Coral. "Mr O is running along the beach. I'd recognise the orange towel anywhere."

"Quick – we must hide inside," ordered Zephyr. And they did, until Mr O had disappeared inside Coral Hut.

"We can't hear. This won't do," whispered Coral with venom.

"You don't have to whisper," replied Nicks. "If we can't hear them, they can't hear us."

"Exactly!" said Coral. "I can't hear them. What good is that? We're supposed to be on a case." She dropped to her haunches and scuttled over to the door of the hut like a two-legged crab. Stretching her neck out like a stalk, she looked left then right. The deck of the hut next door looked clear. Coral turned to her two partners with her thumb raised. "I'll report back," she said in a low voice. And then she was gone, scuttling close to the ground across the red deck and down the stairs, knees and elbows flying.

Nicks and Zephyr turned and blinked at each other. The gold lips moved first.

"We should probably wait here, Binx."

"It's Nicks."

"Sorry."

Coral, meanwhile, had made it undetected to the dark, shadowy space beneath Coral Hut. She paused for a moment and leaned against one of the hut's stilt legs while she got her breath back. As the sound of her heavy breathing subsided, another sound took its place. It was a young man's voice. The floorboards above her head creaked. Somebody fairly heavy was walking across them.

"It's not easy being a role model," said the manly voice, which was definitely Mr O.

"I've done some modelling too," replied the sweeter, higher pitched voice that could only belong to Cecily.

"Was that before you joined the Beach Huts Association?"

There was silence. Coral imagined Cecily nodding (as she had told her to do). But if J.T. was interested in the Association he didn't

133

say anything further. Instead he began telling Cecily all about his training regime for the Olympic triathlon. Cecily sounded interested and made sounds like 'ooh', 'mmm' and 'wow' at strategic places.

Finally J.T. seemed to pause long enough for Cecily to say something. "Would you like some juice?" she asked with a playful tinkle in her voice.

"Is that OJ?" he replied gruffly. "I drink litres of the stuff. It had better not be from concentrate." Coral heard a familiar *pat-pat* sound. And then she remembered; it was the sound of J.T. patting his muscled midriff.

"I've really been looking forward to meeting you," said Cecily happily. Coral listened intently with her head tilted and one ear right by the floorboards above. She could practically hear Cecily batting her eyelashes and swishing her blonde curls this way and that.

"Yeah, and at least you got the breakfast right," replied J.T. "I have to eat healthy to stay at my peak. I'm like a machine." And then there it was again: the familiar *pat-pat* sound. J.T. was flashing his abdominals again.

"I work out," said Cecily in a breathy sort of voice. "I'm a cheerleader."

J.T. chuckled, although not unkindly. "So it's just as well that guys like me give girls like you something to cheer about."

Cecily was silent for a moment. "Uh, isn't this beach hut pretty," she finally replied.

The grunting sound that followed could only have come from J.T. "I guess. But a guy like me is usually carving through the water, pressing the pedals or hitting the road. I don't have time for pretty."

Cecily gave a sudden, shrill squeak but J.T. seemed deaf to anything but his own thoughts.

"Yup," he continued with a lip-smacking sound, "I just gotta keep on moving." The floorboards dipped and creaked double-time. J.T. was obviously giving Cecily a demonstration.

"Would you like something to eat?" she stammered. She sounded lost, like she was not used to her prettiness going unnoticed.

"Sure, I always carbo load after a workout."

"I don't really eat carbohydrates," replied Cecily with the exact same girly giggle that had worked for her so many times in the past. "But then you're so big and strong and I'm quite delicate." Coral heard the sound of material being caressed. Cecily was clearly still in full flirty mode.

"Watch this," replied J.T. And then he made a loud gulping sound. "Can you believe it?"

"Um, no," stuttered Cecily. "I don't think I've ever seen anybody eat a boiled egg that quickly."

"I know – I can practically eat them whole. I've been blessed." There was the sound of more belly patting. "I've always been a high achiever, but my biggest goal is to make the Olympic team. It's what I live for."

There was the sound of Cecily taking deep

breaths – like she still had not come to terms with J.T.'s disinterest in her but was about to give it one final push. "And uh, what else do you like?" she finally asked in a voice that sounded almost desperate.

"I really like—"

"Yes J.T.?" interrupted Cecily, hopefully.

"Canoeing."

Cecily's disappointment was audible. It came whooshing out of her like something deflating.

"It's an impressive sport," added J.T. "Now, that's enough breakfast for me. Thank you and goodbye."

The floorboards creaked one after the other all the way to the door and across the deck. But that was the end of the creaking. Cecily appeared not have moved from her place on the daybed.

"Canoeing," she murmured in a spellbound, high-pitched sort of voice. "It's an impressive sport…"

13

lost and found

Cecily was gone when the Cupid Company returned to Coral Hut. Coral hadn't even heard her leave, but then Cecily was not very heavy under foot. Nicks and Zephyr were eager to hear everything and it took Coral almost ten minutes to tell the story of J.T. and Cecily's blind date, even though it really hadn't turned out to be much of a date after all.

Nicks sighed when Coral was done. "Poor Cecily."

Zephyr and Coral were silent. They also felt a little sorry for the girl, but not for long. The sound of barking quickly distracted them. The trio glanced up and saw Coral's mum with the pups, trekking across the beach in the direction of their hut. Romeo was walking along calmly, but Miss Honey looked flustered and barked intermittently in his ear.

"Hi, girls," shouted Coral's mum in between the shrill yapping.

Coral and Nicks waved and watched and waited until their visitors were close. "Hi, Mum," said Coral. "What's up with Miss Honey?"

Coral's mum shrugged and stared down at the pups. "I don't know. She's been doing that the whole way."

They climbed the steps to the beach hut and had almost reached the top when Romeo stopped and turned to face the beach again. He stared for a long, wistful moment at the stretch of golden sand before him until Miss Honey barked in his ear once again. And then suddenly Romeo was gone, bouncing down the stairs and chugging like a little hairy engine across the sand, until he was nothing more than a small, blurry speck. Coral shouted his name twice, but nothing would bring him back.

"He'll be OK," said Coral's mum. "He loves running on the beach. It's quite safe."

Coral nodded but stared after her pup, perplexed. He'd seemed in a real hurry to get as far away as possible. And then she remembered their new neighbour.

"Oh, Mum, this is Zephyr from the red hut next door," she said.

Coral's mum gave Zephyr a warm Sunday Harbour hug and tried not to stare at the older woman's gold-painted lips. "So where are you from?" she asked instead.

"I'm from nowhere and everywhere," replied Zephyr airily. "I've spent my life travelling, visiting all the weird and wonderful animals and creatures on this planet."

Coral's mum nodded thoughtfully, like she knew exactly what the other woman meant (even though Coral knew that her mum very rarely left Sunday Harbour.) And then suddenly Coral's mum looked really excited about something.

"We're making a real effort with the *Farewell to Summer Beach Party* this year. I hope you'll stay long enough to enjoy it, Zephyr. There's a pie-eating contest as well as sand sculpting and boogie-boarding competitions. We're inviting everyone to contribute to the chalk-art mural that will be drawn on the promenade pavement. And girls – there's an inflatable slide you'll just love! We'll have a bonfire in the evening. And of course we'll build our sand lady. But the big news is that the theatre company will be putting on a very special performance for us all. And guess who's going to be making a guest appearance?"

Suddenly Coral's eyes grew as big and round as planets. "You mean… *us*?" she asked breathlessly.

The smile on her mum's face slipped. "Er, no. It's Tamaran Lancaster!"

Coral and Nicks turned to each other. *Ooooh, the boy who went to our school but is now famous, or he will be when he makes that movie.*

"We'd better try and get his autograph then," replied Nicks.

"Maybe we could help out backstage?" suggested Coral, who firmly believed that having one of the party organisers for a mum should have its perks.

"Maybe," replied her mum, who seemed suddenly distracted. She was fishing about in her jeans pocket with a frown. "There it is," she finally said, holding something shiny in the air.

"Sam's lucky penny!"

"I found it in the washing machine. How many times must I tell you to empty your pockets before you put your clothes in the laundry, Coral?"

"You washed my waistcoat?"

"Of course I did. You don't know where it's been."

Zephyr looked especially interested in the coin, so Coral told her everything.

"Oh, the poor, poor man," replied Zephyr when Coral had finished explaining. "A copper penny is a sign. Sam desperately needs our help, girls. You see, copper is Aphrodite's sacred metal. The goddess of love comes from the island of Cyprus – the greatest source of copper in the ancient world. See what I mean? There is no such thing as coincidence."

"So it's a sign from Aphrodite herself?" murmured Coral with wide eyes. "This makes our mission more important than ever."

Coral's mum coughed. "Well, good luck

143

with that, girls. Now, I need you to take care of the pups for a while – I've got loads to do for the party." She winked and was gone, striding purposefully down the beach.

Coral held the lucky penny up to the sun. They were almost the same size. "It is an unusual coin," she mused. "There can't be many like it in Sunday Harbour. Maybe this is our clue to finding Sam."

"We could place an advert in the Lost and Found section..." began Zephyr.

"... of *The Sunday Harbour Herald*," finished Nicks.

"BRILLIANT!!" cried the girls.

But Miss Honey didn't seem to share their happy mood. She was pacing up and down the deck, pausing every so often to stare out across the empty beach. She didn't look pleased.

"Romeo will be back soon enough," said Coral as she patted the pup's head.

Just then, a bedraggled Cecily appeared,

staggering along the shoreline and dragging a canoe behind her. And Romeo finally returned.

Swaggering across the beach, he mounted the deck stairs one by one, taking his time and pausing to scratch behind one ear with a paw along the way. He passed by Miss Honey without so much as a sniff in her direction. And then he plonked himself down in a warm, sunny spot close to the daybed and promptly fell into a deep, noiseless sleep.

Nicks glanced from Cecily (who was now desperately trying to fasten up her lifejacket and almost strangling herself) to Romeo (who had begun to snore softly) to Miss Honey (whose top lip was curled back in displeasure).

"I think it's very clear," said Nicks, "that we have two rather pressing problems to take care of. Thanks to the Cupid Company, it now appears that Cecily is prepared to go to life-threatening lengths to impress a boy who may just never be very impressed at all. And secondly, I think that the pups are having relationship problems."

Zephyr watched the pups and straightened. "I suggest," she began with an authoritative nod, "that the Cupid Company offers advice and support as an after-sales service."

"I don't think we can worry about that just yet," said Coral. "I think we'd better focus on Cecily first."

Glancing across the sand to where Cecily now stood, apparently trying to launch her canoe into the rolling waves, they couldn't help but notice that the canoe kept tipping over. Now Cecily stepped on the canoe's seat in an attempt to weigh it down. But she was not nearly heavy enough and a wave flipped both girl and canoe over like a pancake. The canoe started floating out to sea and Cecily scrambled after it, peering wildly through a curtain of sodden hair and hanging on to the polka-dot bikini she still appeared determined to wear.

It was not necessary for anyone to speak. The Cupid Company immediately stood up and jogged over to their soggy, half-drowned client.

It had been obvious what Cecily was attempting to do. "Are you sure this is a good idea?" asked Nicks instead.

Cecily stared up at the girls from her place on the sand, mascara streaking down her cheeks. She appeared to have lost one of her sparkly chandelier earrings.

"Canoeing is an impressive sport," she repeated like a dumbstruck robot.

"Er, not always," replied Coral honestly. "Are you OK?"

Cecily nodded and removed a frond of seaweed from her hair. "Sure. I just need to practise. J.T. will be very impressed when he sees that I can canoe."

"Yes, about that," said Coral as she scratched her chin thoughtfully. "Maybe you shouldn't worry too much about trying to impress J.T."

"But of course I must. You were the ones

147

who talked me into finding my one true love, remember?"

Nicks coughed nervously. "Well, there are never any guarantees in this business."

"But you were spot on!" cried Cecily through the sand in her teeth. "I've never felt this way before."

That's because she's never met a boy like J.T. before, thought Nicks.

She's confusing hard-to-get with true love, agreed Coral in silent, best friend mode. *And it's all our fault!*

"I think we should send you on another date, with somebody new," suggested Coral tactfully.

But Cecily shook her head. "No way! You've changed me completely. I am now a one-man woman."

The girls groaned just as another wave lifted the canoe and sent it bashing sideways into Cecily. Losing her balance, she toppled, face-first, into the water. She finally reappeared, squirting water from her mouth like a fountain.

"The girl needs canoeing lessons," murmured Zephyr.

"Very true," gurgled Cecily through saltwater. And then she became very excited indeed. "I know – I'll ask J.T. to teach me how to canoe!"

The girls stared. This had not been their plan, but it was quite obvious that there was no point in protesting.

crazy in love

Plans for the *Farewell to Summer Beach Party* were well underway, thanks to Coral's mum. She was a top organiser and the next day, even offered to place their ad for the lucky penny in the Lost and Found section of the paper. It seemed that even Coral's mum couldn't forget that somewhere in the town of Sunday Harbour an old man sat all alone, waiting to be rescued by the Cupid Company.

This left the girls and Romeo with a morning at the beach, which was already beginning to fill up. It seemed like everyone had the same idea; nobody wanted to miss out on summer's remaining sunshine. But instead of lying about and basking in the warm rays, they all seemed to have things to do.

Small children carried fishing nets and searched for colourful fish and crawling crabs, ready to plop into buckets of saltwater. Old people strolled with their arms tucked behind their backs and admired the blue horizon with a smile. Two teenage boys flew a kite shaped like a giant, red hawk which sent the seagulls scampering. In the distance, the Spikers practised their volleyball in preparation for the big final. They seemed to be working well as a team. And then there was Cecily, sitting calmly beside the orange towel on the beach. She had her canoe with her too.

The girls stood on the deck of Coral Hut

and stared out at a world that seemed to suddenly have slowed down.

J.T. emerged from the waves and leisurely sluiced the water from his arms and legs. Then he slapped his six-pack. Cecily heard the familiar *pat-pat* sound and jumped to her feet. She was wearing a hot-pink bikini with ruffles and had tied a matching scarf in her hair. J.T. seemed surprised to see her. Cecily pointed to the hut while she explained something. The girls dropped instantly to their haunches, but they needn't have worried about being spotted because Cecily was already pointing at her canoe and talking animatedly while J.T. listened with a frown. And then he sighed. And shrugged.

Coral shook her head and disappeared inside the beach hut. She emerged carrying two pairs of dark sunglasses and two peaked caps. "Stick those on your face and pile your hair inside this," she said to Nicks as she handed her glasses and cap. "We're going to

152

have to keep a close eye on Cecily; we may need to step in at some point."

Nicks nodded and went undercover like she'd been told to. And then the girls strolled with casual speed in the direction of the orange towel and hot-pink bikini.

"I suppose I have won the town's Good Role Model Award," they heard J.T. saying. "So it is my duty to pass on my canoeing skills."

Cecily giggled and posed with her feet together. She had one heel raised and her hands clasped neatly in front of her.

J.T. glanced down at her canoe and grunted. "That yours?"

"Uh-huh. Well, it actually belongs to a boy I used to date. I'm looking for true love now though." She paused at this point and fixed a long, hard stare on J.T.

"Is this your first time then?" mumbled J.T., who was still sizing up the canoe.

"Yes," said Cecily. "All the rest were just meaningless flings."

J.T. did not look impressed by the borrowed canoe. "Have you given it a go yet?"

"Nope. But I want to. I yearn for true love. It's become my mission."

"I think we'd better take this one step at a time," continued J.T., like he was the only person there.

Cecily grinned and her eyes shone. "I agree. Much better to take it slowly!"

"We'll have a practice session on the beach first."

Cecily paused for a moment. Confusion flickered across her face. And then she smiled coyly. "Yes, we could hold hands and maybe take a stroll?"

"Here, hold this," J.T ordered. But it wasn't his hand. He shoved a nylon cord with a Velcro looped end in her direction instead. "It's an ankle leash, so that you don't lose your canoe. I'll show you how to put it on."

Cecily giggled and seemed eager to get the flirting back on track, pointing her toe ballerina-style. "You've got such big, strong hands."

J.T. paused and admired his hands for a moment. "Yes, yes I do."

"Do you think I've got a delicate ankle uh, chain?"

"It's called an ankle leash and no, it should never be delicate." J.T. made an impatient 'harrumph' sound, even though Coral and Nicks could quite plainly see the fine silver ankle chain with charms clasped to the end of Cecily's brown, toned calf. "Now, climb into your canoe," he ordered.

Cecily did as she was told.

"I shall now climb in behind you and guide you through the rowing basics."

J.T. kept to his word and edged up closely to Cecily, who tittered and blushed.

"How does this feel?" asked J.T. as he rocked the canoe from side to side.

Cecily sighed. "It just feels so right."

"Yes – left, right, left, right," agreed J.T.

as he rocked sideways some more. "This will help you to work on your balance. Now straighten your spine."

Cecily obeyed and added a flick of her hair for flirty effect. Blonde curls hit J.T. between the eyes and caught in his mouth. Coral and Nicks cringed behind their sunglasses as he gagged and spat out hair. The girls were just about to have a silent, best friend conversation to decide whether Cecily needed rescuing (from herself) when suddenly a sand ball hit Nicks behind the knees. Swinging around, she spied her mum, who was just a few metres away and dusting her hands off with a mischievous grin. Ben was there too and he quickly hid his hand behind his back, like Nicks would never guess that he obviously also had a sand ball that he had been ready to launch.

Nicks groaned. Not only was their timing terrible, but they were behaving like small children. That was the problem with love; it could make once-sensible people act a bit silly. She whispered in Coral's ear and they slipped away without J.T. or Cecily noticing. But they needn't have worried. The canoeists had just tipped headfirst into the sand.

"We're glad we found you," said Nicks's mum with a conspiratorial smile aimed at Ben, who now had Miss Honey instead of a sand ball in his grip. "We weren't sure you'd be at the beach."

"Summer's not over yet!" replied Coral with a grin.

"Miss Honey has been rather down," explained Ben as he cuddled the pup. "At first we thought that maybe she was ill, but now we think she's just missing Romeo."

The girls stared at Miss Honey. She looked more scowling than sad.

"We suspect that the pups have had a falling out—" began Nicks, but she was cut short by a new voice on the scene.

"Halloo halloo," cried Zephyr, her hands in

the air like she'd just crossed a finishing line. And then she noticed the two adults with the girls. "Oh, halloo?"

Coral quickly did the introductions while Nicks's mum and Ben stared at Zephyr's outrageous outfit. Instead of the usual shades of shiny metallic, today's tracksuit was made out of jungle-print fabric and featured tree fronds and leaves with the faces of monkeys, parrots and lizards poking through. The outfit was completed by matching parrot earrings and a green headband stretching across her brown wrinkly forehead.

"So lovely to meet you," declared Zephyr with some more hand waving before turning to face the girls. "I come with an announcement," she said seriously. "I have concocted a three-step relationship programme for the pups. To begin, they'll rediscover why they fell in love in the first place. We'll work through where it's all gone wrong and then establish ways in which they can move forward to a happier, healthier relationship."

"Are you sure you can help them?" asked Coral eagerly. Romeo had spent most of the morning beneath the daybed, which was most unlike him, and Coral was keen to have her pup back to his old self again.

"Maybe they're just not right for each other?" suggested Nicks, who knew enough about love to comment.

Zephyr shrugged and nodded like this was a possibility. "Step one establishes whether their relationship is real love or just loving."

Nicks's mum and Ben stood still, only their heads moving as they followed the conversation like a game of ping-pong. Then Ben frowned. Nicks's mum chuckled and quickly stopped herself. But it was too late; Zephyr had already heard her laugh. The older woman turned to face her.

"The pups are having relationship issues,"

she said sternly. "Love is a primal instinct and it does not matter if you're human or a capybara – that's the world's largest rodent. I know about animals. And love is serious stuff."

Nicks's mum nodded.

"Now," continued Zephyr calmly, "do you think you could leave Miss Honey with us for a bit so that we can begin step one of the programme?"

"Of course," stammered Ben. Nicks's mum nodded some more.

Zephyr clapped her hands. "That's just fabulous!"

desperate times

"Help! HELP! Oh please, you have to help me!"

Coral and Nicks had been lying toe to toe on the daybed and reading copies of *True Love Magazine*. Now they both sat bolt upright. They had been taking a break after a gruelling step-one session with the pups, but suddenly neither felt tired any longer.

"Oh, where are you? PLEASE HELP ME!" cried the voice once again.

The girls turned to the door of Coral Hut, but the background glare meant that they could only see a shape. And the shape, it seemed, had not spied them yet either.

"What's the matter?" called Nicks as she leaped up.

The shape almost fell inside Coral Hut. It was Cecily. She was still wearing the hot-pink ruffled bikini, although she looked rather dishevelled.

"Are you OK?" asked Coral worriedly.

Suddenly Cecily started sobbing loudly. "He thinks I'll never be able to canoe. He said I'm useless."

Of course the girls knew who *he* was. "Who cares what J.T. thinks or says," growled Coral.

Nicks nodded. "Exactly. He's just a self-important... a self-important uh... capybara."

"BUT I LOOOVVE HIM!" cried Cecily with her head thrown back and her fists clenched tight enough to turn her knuckles white.

Coral and Nicks stared at each other. *Love him?* Their faces must have said it all.

"Yes, I love him! You told me to find true love and I have. So now it's the Cupid Company's duty to make him love me back."

"We can't *make* love happen," explained Nicks gently.

"WELL, YOU HAD BETTER FIND A WAY!" roared Cecily. The once tame, pretty and demure young lady had transformed into a raging cyclone that threatened to devour anything that stood in its path to true love.

"OK, just calm down," said Nicks, pacing the beach hut floor and giving it some thought while Cecily's fury dissolved into sobs and she blithered and blubbed about the fact that J.T. thought she was 'very unimpressive'.

"We need a plan. You only have to impress a boy like J.T. once..." murmured Nicks.

"Exactly," agreed Coral. "And I think I know how we can do this. We'll wait for him tomorrow, close to the spot on the beach marked by his orange towel. And Cecily, don't forget to bring your canoe."

"MY CANOE?!" howled Cecily, who seemed to have forgotten how to speak in normal sentences.

"HER CANOE?" cried Nicks, who seemed just as unimpressed by the suggestion.

"Yes, the canoe," confirmed Coral as she calmly exited the hut to survey the beach from the deck. The sun was heading home and so were the beach lovers. It was time for the girls to head back too. She glanced down at the pups, who were snuggled in a corner, finally side by side again. Thanks to Zephyr's step one they seemed to have rekindled the fires of their romance. With the girls' help, Zephyr had artfully re-enacted the moment they had fallen in love. Rubbing noses, cuddling cheek-to-cheek and soft little whines had helped to jog the pups' memories of the event.

Coral tilted her head so that her ears caught the light sea breeze. She could hear something. It was growing louder too. It sounded like... barking. Yes, it was definitely barking. And there was definitely more than one dog too. Romeo did not move much, but the twitch of an ear and a slight twist of his head meant that he'd definitely heard it too. Miss Honey wasn't deaf either, but she did not react at all.

Four excitable, yapping dogs suddenly appeared bounding down the hill from the direction of the promenade. They charged around the corner and finally came to a stop in front of Coral Hut. They sat, quiet and expectant, for a moment. And then they started yapping again. Coral recognised the dogs. They were Romeo's neighbourhood buddies (beach hut lovers were generally dog lovers too).

But still Romeo did not move. Miss Honey did though. She lifted her top lip and growled quietly. Romeo's ear twitched. And then a paw trembled. And then his tail wagged. He couldn't help himself; he was happy to see his friends. But more importantly, he wanted to go seagull chasing with them. It was just what boy dogs did.

The dogs at the bottom of the steps fell silent again and blinked at Romeo expectantly. Nobody moved for a while. And then Miss Honey stood up, heaved a great big sigh, and slowly ambled inside Coral Hut without so much as a backward glance.

It was now up to Romeo. Standing up on shaky knees, he blinked back at his mates. And then, with his tail between his legs, he slowly turned and followed Miss Honey indoors.

Coral stood staring after her pup, wondering if step one in Zephyr's programme had been such a good idea after all. She loved Romeo and wanted him to see him happy. After all, wasn't being happy what true love was really all about?

can-oe!

The girls knew J.T.'s training schedule well enough by now to plan their timing perfectly. And of course it did not take them very long to find his bright orange towel on the beach. Cecily arrived with her canoe. They were just about ready to launch. Almost.

"Do you think that's an appropriate outfit for canoeing?" Coral asked Cecily. Today's bikini was a boob tube with dangling brown and cream shells sewn into the seams. She also wore a matching cowry shell necklace and hooped earrings.

Cecily glanced down at her outfit and frowned. "You don't think the shells are beachy enough?" she asked nervously.

"No, it's beachy..." Coral shrugged and then gave up.

"What exactly is your plan?" Nicks asked Coral.

"My plan," she began, turning to Cecily, "is for you to impress J.T. To do that you'll either have to qualify for the Olympics or learn to canoe like a pro – in like the next ten minutes."

"We know she can't do either," interrupted Nicks impatiently.

Cecily's shoulders sagged.

Coral grinned.

"True, she'll never qualify for the Olympics. But with our help Cecily can *look* like a pro canoeist. Now we don't have much time – J.T.

will almost have finished his swim. Cecily, you'd better hop into the canoe now."

Cecily and Nicks looked confused.

"Come on!" urged Coral. "You've got to be in the water for this to work."

So Cecily did as she was told. She jingled as she walked – bikini shells clonking musically.

"Slide your feet into the canoe's foot straps," ordered Nicks sensibly.

Cecily smiled down at her feet. "I painted my toes especially."

"Yes, that's nice," murmured Coral as she handed her the oar. "Now, we're going to push you into the water slowly, OK? Try to remain upright."

Cecily nodded nervously. "I wish this thing had a seatbelt."

"Not if you capsize, you won't," replied Nicks.

"Just stay calm and don't jiggle about," ordered Coral while the girls gently pushed the canoe until the front end touched the water. The back end soon followed and almost immediately Cecily started to panic.

"Just sit still," called Coral.

"Is this really a good idea?" whispered Nicks. "You know she can't do this."

"She can if we help her. Now just keep pushing until the water reaches your chest."

"We're going in too?"

"Of course we are." And then Coral spoke to Cecily. "We'll be here with you all the time, all right?"

Cecily nodded, but looked a little pale.

"When we're deep enough, Nicks and I will angle the canoe so that you're parallel to the beach. We'll hide on the other side of the canoe, but we won't let you go. Then, when J.T. heads for his towel, you'll call out loudly to him and pretend you're canoeing. And we'll push you along, so that it looks like you're actually canoeing and in control."

Cecily thought about this and then

grinned. "Ooh, that will make me look good. And then what?"

Coral frowned and bit her lip. She hadn't really thought it through any further than that.

"There's J.T.!" cried Cecily in a gravelly whisper.

"Oh my goodness!" gasped Nicks (tensions were high and the water was rather chilly).

"Quick, he mustn't see us!" snapped Coral. "Nicks – push!"

They pushed. The canoe tilted and Cecily squealed. Small waves created by the canoe sloshed up the noses of the two girls in the water and into their mouths. Nicks coughed.

"Would you both keep it down," choked Coral.

"I'll try and drown quietly," snapped Nicks, who did not like this plan one bit.

"Cecily, pretend you're canoeing and call out to J.T.", instructed Coral once the canoe had steadied.

"Should I fix my hair first?"

"No, you shouldn't!" growled Nicks.

"J.T. – yoohoo!" Cecily called out while she pretended to canoe. Of course Nicks and Coral only had a close-up view of a side of the canoe, but they didn't hear him call back. "I don't think he heard me," whispered Cecily after a few moments.

"Shout louder this time," replied Coral as she dodged a swipe of the oar.

"J.T. – hiya!"

But still he did not seem to hear her.

"Much louder," insisted Coral, who was also quickly tiring of this plan (and of close-calls with the dipping oar).

"HEY, J.T! LOOK AT ME!" roared Cecily at the top of her voice. It wasn't just J.T. who paid attention now.

"WOW! IT LOOKS LIKE YOU'RE ACTUALLY CANOEING!" J.T. shouted back loud enough to be heard.

Cecily started laughing manically. "I KNOW – INSANE!" And then she glanced down at the two girls still holding the canoe and desperately pushing it along while waves lapped at their chins. "He gave me the thumbs up!" she whispered excitedly. "He seemed impressed too."

"Don't look at us – just keep on canoeing!" said Nicks.

Cecily turned back to J.T. "THERE'S NOTHING TO IT – EASY PEASY!" she chanted as she canoed. The canoe was moving forward but of course J.T. wasn't. Not that this mattered. They had achieved their goal. Their mission had been successful.

"Now say goodbye, Cecily," ordered Coral.

"SEE YOU AROUND VERY SOON, J.T.!" she hollered and waved with the oar. Luckily the girls still had a firm grip on the canoe.

"Is he leaving the beach now?" whispered Nicks hoarsely. It felt like she'd swallowed a lot of the ocean.

"Nope, he's just standing there, watching me," replied Cecily happily.

"I'm sure he'll pick up his towel and leave," gasped Coral.

"He'd better do it soon," groaned Nicks.

"He's still standing there," said Cecily, still smiling.

"And now?"

"Nope, he's still there," replied Cecily.

The girls kept pushing the canoe forward. "What about now?"

Cecily shook her head.

"Surely now?"

"He's still watching."

"Mind that oar, Cecily!"

"Sorry."

"Has he even picked up his towel yet?"

"Doesn't look like it."

"It seems like your plan worked a little too well," moaned Nicks, who was beginning to wonder if they'd end up circumnavigating the globe, J.T. watching and Cecily waving her oar like the Queen, while the two girls pushed the canoe with their wrinkly fingers.

17

PUPPY love

Nicks soon forgave Coral. She even offered to share her bar of chocolate when Coral and Romeo arrived at her house the following day. Both visitors smiled. Coral was pleased that her friend seemed to have forgotten about the day before and Romeo looked visibly relieved to find that Miss Honey was out with Ben and Nicks's mum.

"I think I've finally dried out," Nicks grumbled with a half-smile.

"Saltwater is good for you," replied Coral as she helped herself to another square of her friend's chocolate bar.

"Swimming in it, maybe, but not swallowing half an ocean."

Coral shrugged and nodded. "Yes, it might be an idea to stay away from salty snacks for the next few days. Anyway, I have some very good news."

"What, no more of your crazy ideas?"

But Coral just grinned and waved a piece of paper in the air. "Mum just gave me this: two people have responded to our ad for the lucky penny."

Nicks brightened instantly. "Two? Oh, brilliant!" One of these was bound to be Sam.

Coral slapped the piece of paper down on the table. Both girls stared at the two names alongside the telephone numbers.

"'Jett' and 'Penny Princess'?" Nicks read out loud.

Coral sighed. "I'm sure one of them will know Sam."

Nicks did not look convinced but dialled the first number anyway. The phone rang six times.

"So yeah, like, hello, this is Jett."

"This is Nicks calling about the lucky penny we found."

"Coolio! Like, my lucky penny."

"The penny is yours?" Nicks tried not to sound disappointed.

"Like, definitely."

"Erm, but do you know Sam?"

"I like, guess so. Everyone knows a Sam, right?"

Nicks shrugged. This was probably true. "But do you know Sam who drives a Morris Minor and wears waistcoats and is probably an actor?"

There was a short silence at the other end of the phone. "Sounds like a cool dude."

Nicks harrumphed. "So you don't know him?"

"Guess not, dudette."

And then it occurred to Nicks. "Are you sure we have *your* lucky penny?"

"Def-o!"

"Can you describe it for me?"

"Like, sure. So it has like, two sides."

"And?"

"It's all shiny."

"Yes?"

"An' round."

"I'm going to need more."

"It's like, silver."

"Silver?"

"I mean, gold. Like, goldy."

"And what about the pictures on the coin?"

"Yeah, they're so cool."

"No, I mean, can you describe it."

"Shew – I have a terrible memory, man."

"Jett?"

"Like, yeah?"

178

"I don't think we have your lucky penny after all."

"You don't?"

"Nope, I'm afraid not."

"Oh bummer, dudette, I really could do with some good luck."

"Goodbye, Jett."

Nicks hung up the phone and shook her head. And then she got busy dialling the other number on the notepaper. This time the phone only rang once.

"This is Penny."

"Penny as in Penny Princess?" asked Nicks.

Suddenly Penny's voice changed. It became deeper. She spoke slower and with a sense of importance. "This is *the* Penny Princess, yes."

"Apparently you think we have your lucky penny," said Nicks who wasn't quite as quick to part with the penny second time round.

"Oh no, it's not my lucky penny, it's yours."

"Mine?"

"Yes, that's why I called you. I know a thing

179

or two about lucky pennies. You could say that it is my specialist subject. And the rule is finder's keepers. Copper is an excellent conductor of luck, and good luck is meant to be passed on – that's how it works. But you can't pass the good luck back, that is – you can't give a lucky penny back."

"So you don't know Sam then?" mumbled Nicks.

"Sam?"

"I didn't think so. Thanks Penny, uh, Princess."

"Remember what I said."

"Sure, will do."

"Ching ching."

"Pardon?"

"That's the sound of the lucky penny. It brings more good luck. I know these things."

Nicks groaned, although they would probably need this extra luck. "OK, thanks. Bye."

"Ching chi—"

But Nicks had already put the phone down. Her mum and Ben arrived home at exactly the same moment. Miss Honey was with them but trailed a little way behind. She had not been built for speed.

"I'm sure the penguins will sort it out," said Nicks's mum to Ben, who simply sighed deeply and ran a hand through his dark hair. He looked concerned.

"What's up with the penguins?" asked Nicks.

Ben sighed once more before answering. "The penguins' breeding programme is very important to the aquarium, but this is the second breeding season where we haven't seen any new chicks. It's all quite worrying."

Nicks's mum gave Ben a hug. "Oh, Cuddly Bun, they'll work it out."

Ben smiled at her affectionately. "Thanks, Sweet Cheeks."

Coral and Nicks stared at each other and had a silent, best friend conversation.

Cuddly Bun?

Sweet Cheeks?

Seriously gross.

Definitely!

Coral imagined her parents calling each other lovey-dovey nicknames and shuddered.

Romeo may have heard the others return but he stayed in his corner and pretended to sleep. Of course Miss Honey sniffed him out. She waddled over, stood in front of him and gave a single, sharp bark. Romeo lifted an eyelid and stared at her. Then he stood up, shifted over five inches and flopped back down again. Miss Honey quickly nestled into his warm space and promptly fell fast asleep with an ear draped over Romeo's snout. His little black nose wrinkled and his big brown eyes watered. And then he growled softly. Miss Honey woke instantly. Romeo had never growled at her before. She raised her tail and whacked him. She then whacked him once more, for good measure. Romeo sat upright and growled a little louder, but he was quickly drowned out by Miss Honey, who answered him with a stream of infuriated, high-pitched yaps.

Everyone heard their argument and frowned with concern.

"The pups need to get out," said Nicks's mum. "Won't you girls take them for a walk?"

They had to do something. Nicks nodded and Coral reached for the leads. They didn't mind going for a walk one bit, especially not with all the Cuddly Bun-Sweet Cheeks conversation about. Of course love rocked at any age, but parents were still supposed to behave like parents!

The beachfront was busy and colourful too, and with more than just people. The girls noticed the new posters at exactly the same time. They were big and bright and attached to lampposts, walls and railings.

"The *Farewell to Summer Beach Party*," read Nicks. "And thanks to the Cupid Company, there's the volleyball final to look forward to."

"And look there," cooed Coral as she pointed to the name printed in large red and silver letters. "We're going to see Tamaran Lancaster in action. Eeek!"

They weren't the only ones delighted at the thought of Tamaran Lancaster visiting the seaside town, and every now and again there came a new girly shriek as another fan spied his name on the posters.

The pups were still ignoring each other, so the girls continued on to the row of beach huts. That's when they noticed something different about their neighbouring red beach hut. Today it had a wooden FOR SALE sign tied to the deck.

Zephyr arrived at that precise moment. She continued up the deck steps, past

184

the FOR SALE sign and put her key in the door.

Nicks turned to Coral. "I wonder if Zephyr will buy the hut."

"Course she will!" cried Coral, who was instantly very excited at the thought of having a creative animal lover with a futuristic fashion sense for a permanent beach hut neighbour. Zephyr waved and then continued struggling with the door lock, which appeared to be stiff. Coral stuck her head through the deck railings. "So you're buying the hut then?"

"Erm, probably not," replied Zephyr as she rammed the jammed door with her hip.

"I'm sure you can get the door fixed quite easily," suggested Nicks, who had grown fond of Zephyr (even if the old lady could never get her name right).

Finally Zephyr seemed to forget about the door. She smiled warmly at Nicks. "It's not the hut, but thanks, Micks. I'm just not convinced I'm ready to settle down yet and make Sunday Harbour my final destination. It's a difficult decision."

The girls turned to each other and had a silent, best friend conversation.

It's obvious that Zeph is lonely.

I think she tries not to think about it.

Maybe she doesn't realise how old she's getting.

Zephyr definitely needs to settle down.

"But Sunday Harbour needs you," said Coral with passion.

"Exactly," added Nicks. "I mean, what would the pups do without you?"

All three glanced down at Romeo and Miss Honey, who were now rumbling fiercely at each other while Miss Honey continued to give Romeo regular whacks of her tail between the eyes. Zephyr's three-step relationship programme didn't appear to be doing much good. But then, as agents of love, the girls both knew that sometimes love just wasn't meant to be.

"OK, so forget about the pups," continued Nicks, "but the aquarium desperately needs you; there hasn't been a penguin chick born there for two years."

Coral grinned at her friend with a face that said *GENIUS!*

"No chicks for two years?" murmured Zephyr thoughtfully. "But penguins usually always form faithful breeding pairs. They live in happy little families with both parents helping to look after the babies."

"Not at the Sunday Harbour Aquarium they don't," replied Coral happily, like this was a good thing.

"It is a compelling mystery," replied Zephyr as she tapped her chin. "Do you think I could pay the penguins a visit?"

"I'm sure of it," said Nicks. "Nobody knows animal relationships like you do."

Coral was very pleased that Zephyr now

had the penguins to focus on. Of course she didn't want their neighbour to leave, but she also secretly hoped that Romeo might avoid step two of the programme. Love was supposed to bring happiness; that was its job. And Romeo did not look happy one bit.

the best laid plans

With only a few days left before the *Farewell to Summer Beach Party* and the volleyball final, the Spikers were out in full force. They exercised on the beach. They huddled in tight circles and practised invigorating war cries. Rory, the captain, paced up and down as he outlined manoeuvres and detailed strategies to the rest of his teammates. And of course they practised, practised and practised some more until they gleamed with perspiration.

Cecily was spending a lot more time at the beach too, but these days this had nothing to do with the Spikers. It had nothing to do with her role as head cheerleader either, although the cheerleaders had been doing some practising of their own. But they held their practice sessions in secret; it was important to them that nobody heard their cheerleading chants until the big event. But with no scheduled cheerleading practice session, Cecily was back at the beach. Coral and Nicks watched her wandering up and down the water's edge. It was impossible to tell if she was happy in love and the girls could not resist finding out.

"Hi, Cecily," said Nicks.

"So have you seen J.T. again?" asked Coral in her usual direct manner.

Cecily shook her head. "Not yet, but he usually arrives about now."

190

Like the Cupid Company, she'd obviously also got to know his training routine very well.

And true to form, he arrived exactly on schedule, running along the beach, clutching the ends of the bright orange towel which was draped around his neck. He spied the girls and slowed. He looked especially pleased to see Cecily. Coral and Nicks turned to each other and grinned. Would this be another success story for the Cupid Company?

Cecily was clearly still very taken with J.T. She smiled coyly at him and curled her hair around her finger while she doodled random shapes in the damp sand with her big toe.

"Hello, Cecily," said J.T. with bright eyes.

"Hi, J.T." Twirl. Twirl. Doodle. Doodle.

"I was hoping I'd bump into you. I have something to tell you."

Cecily's face lit up like Guy Fawkes Night. "Oh, J.T. – I feel the same!" she cried out happily.

"You do? Oh good – but er, how did you know I'd signed you up for the Canoe Club?"

"The Canoe Club!" cried all three girls at once.

J.T. looked very pleased with himself, or more pleased than usual, anyway. "Yes, the Canoe Club. I have called in a few favours. It's not usually a club for beginners, but you are talented. You were canoeing like a pro after only one lesson on the sand! That's not bad going. So they're expecting you at the clubhouse tomorrow morning at six sharp."

The girls stood there in gobsmacked silence.

"I know, it's pretty great," continued J.T. after a while. "You're probably thinking I'm pretty great too. I guess it's the sort of thing that wins me role model awards, so no need to thank me."

"OK, good," murmured Cecily dismally. And then she turned to Coral. There was no mistaking her scowl. Nicks was scowling too.

Coral sensed that this was probably not the time for long-winded explanations so she stood quietly with a flat, hard grin pasted to her face.

J.T. was silent too. And when it became apparent that no one was going to praise or applaud him, he gripped his orange towel even tighter and prepared for take-off.

"I've got a workout to complete. Cecily, good luck with the Canoe Club." And then he was gone.

Coral finally breathed. "Now Cecily, as crusaders of love, I think the time has come for us to accept that J.T. might not be the one for you. There's no making something out of something that isn't."

"BUT WHAT ABOUT FINDING TRUE LOVE?!" wailed Cecily, so loudly that people turned to look.

"True love is still out there," explained Nicks gently.

"BUT I WANT TO BE LOVED AND ADORED!"

Coral and Nicks thought about this. *Yes, that's what it always comes back to: Cecily wanting to be adored.*

Cecily sniffed and glanced over at the Spikers practising at the other end of the beach. She seemed to be contemplating things.

"No, no, just look away!" cried Nicks, who knew exactly what Cecily was thinking.

"I'm not sure you're much of a Cupid Company at all," grumbled Cecily miserably. "I've gone from having lots of boyfriends to absolutely none at all." And then she started wailing.

"Oh, please don't make that sound," pleaded Nicks, who did not like to draw attention to herself (and people really were staring).

"Yes, it'll all be OK," cooed Coral tenderly. But it seemed to make no difference to the wailing.

"Cecily, belt up!" ordered Nicks firmly and with authority. "You simply can't have lots of boyfriends – it's not right. That's not what

194

love and romance is about. Now, all hope is not lost. *I* will come up with a plan!" She looked pointedly at Coral.

"When?" sniffed Cecily.

"When the time is right!" declared Nicks in a forthright manner that was quite unlike her. "But for now, you need to march over to the Canoe Club and withdraw your membership because let's face it, you're bright and pretty and a very nice girl but canoeing is *not your thing*."

Cecily nodded, sniffed once more and finally shuffled off.

"Don't worry, she'll be OK," said Nicks coolly. "Our next order of business is Romeo."

"He should not do step two in the programme!" gasped Coral.

Nicks nodded. "Definitely agreed. Miss Honey is not the pup for him. It was a flash in the pan. It was a fun fling, but they are not suited. Now we have to distract Romeo so that he can move on as painlessly as possible."

Coral nodded silently. She was in awe of the newly confident Nicks. It seemed like everything going wrong had brought out the true strength in her friend.

Nicks stared at the Spikers for what seemed like an age. And then she punched the salty air with her small fist. "Follow me!" she cried out. "The Spikers are about to get a mascot – Romeo!"

summer's winter

The Spikers were delighted to have Romeo as their mascot (or if they weren't they were too terrified to say no to the bold and brazen Nicks, who was now more take-charge than ever).

"With that agreed..." said Nicks, her pen pointed at the lined paper pinned to her foil butterfly clipboard, "...we must now find

Romeo something blue to wear. A little royal blue scarf might look nice."

"And I could paint the name STRIKERS on it," suggested Coral.

"Good idea," said Nicks as she jotted this bit of information down. "Now, about the *Farewell to Summer Beach Party*: I think that the Cupid Company should capitalise on the event. Winter is not far away and those long, cold nights can seem endless. So we should make the party look as romantic as possible. Nobody wants to be alone, especially not during winter."

Coral smiled. "I like it! How about paper lanterns with scented candles? And there's my box of heart-shaped decorations. I'll talk to my mum – she'll love the idea."

Nicks made a 'mmm' sound as she wrote. Finally she glanced up. "That just leaves Sam. Will we ever find him, I wonder?"

"Everyone in Sunday Harbour comes to the *Farewell to Summer Beach Party*," mused

Coral. "Nobody would miss it. That means Sam will be there, somewhere in the crowd."

"Yes, true. So now our only job is to find him."

The girls thought about this. *This had pretty much been their job all along, only now his location would be narrowed down, which would be some help.*

"It'll be our last chance to find him, I think," concluded Nicks. "But we're not quite done yet. What about Zephyr?"

"We can't let her leave Sunday Harbour," said Coral.

"Yup, this is the best seaside town on the planet. She couldn't possibly be happier – or less lonely – anywhere else." Finally Nicks removed her nose from her clipboard. "We must go and see how she's getting on with the penguins. Maybe they'll be able to convince her to stay."

Nicks was on a roll and Coral was happy to follow her lead. And thanks to Ben, the girls were able to walk right into the aquarium without queuing first. Of course they knew exactly where to find the penguins, which meant that they knew exactly where to find Zephyr, although for once she was not easy to spot. Today she had on a black and white satin tracksuit. She matched the penguins perfectly.

The girls sidled up to the enclosure railings and watched quietly for a few moments. Zephyr was sitting in the middle of the penguin colony. She barely stirred and spoke even less. Her eyes narrowed as she quietly observed the mammals. And then, just when it seemed that she might never do anything at all, she finally moved. She stood up, her arms held straight and pressed to her sides, and waddled penguin-style over to Ben, who stood waiting at the canopied entrance to the enclosure. The girls moved their legs double-time to join them.

"Hi, girls," said Zephyr when she saw them. But she looked distracted and turned to stare at the penguins again. And then she cleared her throat. "Ben, were your penguins born in this aquarium?"

"No, as a matter of fact they weren't," Ben replied.

Zephyr scratched her chin. "That's your problem. The penguins are homesick." She looked wistful and spoke in a whisper. "Home is a very special place. Everyone needs one." And then she seemed to snap out of it, becoming businesslike once again. "Ben, these penguins are wary and unsettled. They need some reassurance that this is where they belong."

"And how do we do that?" asked Ben.

"We make this place look more like home," replied Zephyr.

"And how do we do that?" Ben repeated.

Zephyr stared past her penguin outfit at her feet. When she finally spoke it was like she was thinking out loud. "We create fake icebergs and craggy white peaks. All these trees really must go; they have no place in Antarctica. White, open space – that's what the penguins need to feel more at home."

Ben coughed. "Yes, erm, thanks for the advice, but while these penguins weren't born in our aquarium, they weren't *actually* born in Antarctica either."

Zephyr sent him a withering look. "I understand that, Ben. But it's all to do with primitive instincts and memories, you see. All this brown concrete and shrubbery is just too foreign to these creatures. And it's distracting them from what they usually do very well – that is, raising little families. It's like white noise, interfering with their primal intuition."

Ben gave this some thought. And then he shrugged and nodded like the suggestion wasn't half bad after all. "OK, but I'm not sure we have the resources to create this winter wonderland you describe."

Coral and Nicks, who up until now had

remained silent, shifted uncomfortably. Nothing was impossible as far as they were concerned. And Nicks was still as determined as ever.

"Well, actually," she said out loud, "there is one way we could do it. The Sunday Harbour Theatre Company is always creating imaginative stage sets. I bet their stage designers would know exactly how to build a winter wonderland in the middle of Sunday Harbour's aquarium."

Zephyr actually cried out loud with happiness. "Jinx – that is a truly brilliant idea!"

Nicks rolled her eyes but the others looked very impressed. "If it means there's a chance that we can finally see our first penguin chick born in the aquarium, then it's got to be worth a go," agreed Ben. "We have a budget for that sort of thing."

Zephyr gleamed. "So it's set."

"We have to get the theatre company to

agree to take on the project first," replied Ben seriously. "I'd better make the phone call. After all, it is my job."

"You can do it!" shouted Coral, who was suddenly overcome by the excitement of it all. And then she hugged her very smart, very best friend in the world. They had so much to look forward to. The romance-themed *Farewell to Summer Beach Party* was just around the corner. And very soon they would have lots of little penguin families to *ooh* and *ahh* at. It really would be love all around.

20

SAM1

The next few days flew by in a bright blur of colours and sounds. Preparations for the big party were already well underway. Stalls with striped canopies grew out of frames and canvas. Men in overalls climbed poles secured with ropes and pulleys and strung wire for the speaker system. A marquee covered the row of small tables for the panel of judges who would be overseeing the various contests.

Further away, a bit closer to the water's edge, the people of Sunday Harbour contributed logs and sticks to a pile for the evening bonfire. And right in the centre of everything stood a flat, raised platform. It was where they would have their very own theatre-in-the-round. This was exactly where Tamaran Lancaster would stand and move about. His actual feet were going to touch those ordinary, rather mundane planks of wood. The girls stared at the planks like they were other-worldly. They soon would be.

"What are you two doing just standing about?" hooted Coral's mum, who was scampering about as usual, fretting about To Do lists and people to see. "I need your help. Girls, do you think you could mark out the area for the inflatable slide?"

"We'd like to," replied Coral, even though they'd been helping all morning, "but we've got to get over to the aquarium. It's very important."

Coral's mum sighed but nodded like she understood. "OK, but make sure you're back in time to hang your special decorations. I've got the scented candles and lanterns all ready for you." She winked at the girls. She loved love almost as much as they did.

Nicks saluted and grinned. "Will do!"

"We really still have quite a lot to do," Coral's mum called out. But the girls were already racing for the stairs to the promenade. They were so excited. Today was a very big day. The theatre company's head set designer was making a personal visit to the aquarium. Of course Zephyr and Ben would be there, but the girls had been invited along too. After all, some of it was their idea.

The aquarium's parking lot was always busy. Not that the girls really noticed; all they could think about was baby penguins. They raced past the cars and into the main entrance, where Steven the Starfish waved them through with a friendly smile. They had almost reached the Touch Tank when Nicks suddenly came to a screeching halt. She stood very still, breathing heavily and staring at the floor with faraway eyes.

"What's the matter, are you all right?" asked Coral, prodding her friend's shoulders and arms. Nicks certainly felt OK.

"I think we missed something," puffed Nicks. "In the parking lot... Follow me!"

So Coral did. She trailed Nicks until they were standing back at the entrance to the aquarium, overlooking the parking lot. "Look there," said Nicks in amazement. She pointed and stared with big eyes, like a two-headed alien had just landed in front of her.

And there it was – a Morris Minor parked in the bay closest to the aquarium entrance. They had raced straight past it.

The girls took tentative steps forward, their mouths open wide. They were mesmerised; it might as well have been a two-headed alien in front of them. The car had a black body and a white roof with matching whitewall tyres. And the number plate said: SAM1.

Finally the girls managed to move. They stared at each other and had a silent, best friend conversation.

I do not believe it.

I don't think I can even speak, like ever again.

But this is TOPS!

Yes, definitely tops. Aphrodite is clearly watching over us.

"Sam is not an actor but apparently the theatre's head set designer," whispered Nicks. It was a revelation.

"We found Sam!" cried Coral with a little more oomph.

"Yes, *we* really did! After all, it was our idea to call on the theatre company to build the winter wonderland."

"We rock."

"Yes Coral, yes we do."

The girls marched calmly in the direction

of the penguin enclosure. And there was Sam. The girls stared at him like he was a vision. They'd spent so much time and effort searching for him and now here he was, quite unexpectedly. He almost didn't seem real, which was exactly why they could not stop staring at him.

Sam was a short man with a soft belly and white hair that matched his white beard. He was smartly dressed with red braces over a white shirt and on his head he wore a hat with a single feather. He looked kind and jolly and interesting. He looked a bit like Santa's eccentric younger brother.

"There you are!" called Ben when he spotted the girls. "Come and meet Sam."

Come and meet Sam. If only Ben knew just how hard the girls had been trying to do this.

"How are you, Sam?" said Nicks with a hand politely extended.

"Yes, *just how are you?*" repeated Coral. "Have you been coping?"

"With what?" asked a slightly confused-looking Sam.

"With life, Sam," replied Coral as she stared into his eyes, which were slightly watery, but that was probably because he was a bit old.

"Yes, I cope with life very well, thank you," said Sam.

"I'm Amor. And this is Nicks. That's good to hear, Sam. So you haven't been too lonely then?"

Nicks stared ahead with a frozen smile and side-kicked Coral's shins.

Sam smiled and really did not seem put-out. "Nope, not lonely at all. But thanks for your concern."

Ben, meanwhile, looked really puzzled. He coughed loudly. "Now, about the winter wonderland..."

"But where is Zephyr?" asked Nicks.

Ben checked his watch. "She should've been here already."

Suddenly, and as if on cue, Zephyr arrived,

breathless and panting. "Sorry I'm late, one and all," she declared with a dramatic wave of her hands, "but there's been the most awful situation. You see, I've been keenly observing a most beautiful swan couple who've made the pond their home. I've called them Odette and Siegfried and they are doting parents to three of the most adorable cygnets... well, there were six actually, but only three of the babies survived. And then yesterday Siegfried flew too close to a power line. It left him disorientated and terrified and he's since refused to go near Odette and the little ones. But swans are tranquil, faithful, and committed to family and the raising of young. I knew it was temporary – Siegfried just needed a little help. They have kept me busy!"

Finally Zephyr stopped talking and drew a deep breath. Everyone stared. Her extraordinary story was only matched by her outfit: today's tracksuit was entirely purple and shiny with a wide belt encrusted with knuckle-sized, coloured-glass gems. The look was completed by a much smaller gem which she'd glued between her eyebrows.

Sam was the first to speak. "How very interesting," he murmured.

"It is an interesting story," agreed Coral.

"Yes, the story too..." added Sam distractedly.

Of course the girls saw it. The recognised the signs. They weren't the Cupid Company for nothing. The girls nudged each other and began a silent, best friend conversation.

Are you thinking what I'm thinking?

Two lovebirds...

... and one arrow from Cupid's bow?

Definitely!

"Sam, this is Zephyr. And Zephyr, this man is called Sam," rhymed Coral without actually meaning to. "You'll probably need to spend quite a lot of time together, planning the penguins' winter wonderland."

Zephyr smiled a Broadway sort of smile

and extended her hand, which Sam accepted with a light kiss. The girls shrugged: old people did things differently. It was a good start. Sam then hooked his arm through Zephyr's and the two began walking.

"Now, dear, you must tell me all about your ideas for a winter wonderland..." the girls heard Sam say as the pair ambled in the direction of the penguin enclosure.

Ben, Coral and Nicks watched them for a few moments. And then Ben sighed.

"The older generation has such a romantic way of doing things," he said.

The girls turned to Ben and frowned. They scrunched up their faces and hunched their shoulders. They were trying to make it very clear that lovey-dovey stuff was not for everyone. *Parents were still supposed to behave like parents* (and not like Cuddly Buns or Sweet Cheeks!).

hearty party

It wasn't easy for the girls to focus on plans for the *Farewell to Summer Beach Party* after this. Of course they couldn't wait for it, but they were distracted by the exciting developments in the penguin enclosure at the aquarium. Sam and Zephyr had been working together – sharing ideas, sketching diagrams and reviewing building materials and paint. With so much going on, it really wasn't surprising that the morning of the beach party seemed to arrive sooner than expected. It was the most beautiful day too – almost as if summer knew that it had to leave soon and was determined to make one last, spectacular effort before then.

Coral and Romeo woke early and had a good breakfast. Coral then dressed Romeo in his special royal blue bandanna painted with the name STRIKERS. He didn't seem to mind wearing it one bit. In fact, it was almost as if he understood exactly what being a mascot was all about. He stood tall and proud and panted with his pink tongue hanging out. Coral smiled and reached for her waistcoat. She'd been saving it for this day. *Sam would be surprised.* This reminded her. She removed the lucky penny from its safe place and dropped it into the waistcoat's satin-lined pocket.

"I think we're about ready," she then murmured to her pup. Romeo replied with a loud bark.

Coral's mum had already left for the beach. The house was quiet without her around so there was no missing the soft, polite knock at the bedroom door.

"Yes, Dad?" said Coral.

The door opened. "Nicks is here," he said calmly. And sure enough, there was Nicks.

Coral's father was about to close the door but seemed to change his mind at the last minute. He stuck his head into the room again.

"You see," he said, "it *is* possible to communicate in this house without yelling from one end to the other." And then he was gone.

"It's not the same without your mum hollering my name from the front door," said Nicks.

Coral chuckled along with her friend. "What do you think about Romeo's mascot outfit?" she then asked.

"It's tops. I do like your waistcoat too."

"Really?"

"Well, sort of – mostly."

Coral made for the door. "You won't find another like it," she said over her shoulder and grinned.

The girls heard the party before they actually saw it – even though they were early. It wasn't quite noon yet, but already the place was churning with organisers and stall owners and some very eager party guests. Everywhere looked colourful and cheery and matched the steady stream of people arriving.

"Our heart-shaped decorations definitely add that special romantic touch," commented Nicks as she gazed around her in wonder.

"Look there!" cried Coral suddenly. "It's Charlie. And she's holding Jake's hand."

"You mean Charlie as in Birdie and the Captain's daughter?"

"Yes, there!" Coral jiggled her pointing finger for emphasis.

Finally Nicks saw them. Charlie and Jake

were quite clearly still a very happy couple –
thanks to the Cupid Company. The girls smiled.
They hadn't seen their old Cupid Company
clients for some time; it was good to know that
they were still very much in love.

"We'll definitely say hello later, but first we
really should get Romeo over to the Spikers.
After all, what is a volleyball team without
the best mascot in the world!"

Romeo barked like he couldn't agree more.
Coral nodded. There was so much to see and
do, but they had to prioritise.

The Sunday Harbour cheerleaders had
arrived too. The group of six girls were
dressed up in pretty pleated skirts with royal
blue pom-poms for shaking. They grinned
like their big day had finally arrived... all
except for one of them. Cecily's face did not
match her cheery outfit. Her shoulders were
slumped and she seemed to be scowling... at
all the heart decorations.

She saw the girls approaching and slumped

down further. "I suppose *those*," she snapped as she pointed to the hearts, "are courtesy of the Cupid Company?"

"Well, erm…" mumbled Coral, who was suddenly vaguely nervous of no-boyfriend-Cecily. "Those are just silly paper hearts." This was not easy for Coral to say; there was nothing silly about hearts but she didn't like to see Cecily miserable either.

"Cheer up, Cecily," said Nicks kindly.

"HOW CAN I CHEER UP?" wailed Cecily. "This is the biggest day of a cheerleader's calendar and I don't have a boyfriend to watch me from the sidelines. *What is the point!*"

"The point is the Spikers," replied Nicks, who was still taking no nonsense. "We're here to support our volleyball team, remember?"

But Cecily just growled and stomped off.

"I don't think we should leave Romeo with her," whispered Coral to her friend.

"I see Jem and Em," replied Nicks. "He'll be in good hands with them."

Romeo was happy to be handed over. In fact, he looked taller and grander than ever. Strutting along, his little barrel chest was all puffed out and his tail pointed straight at the sky. And then the girls saw them: the four beach hut pups – Romeo's neighbourhood mates. They were watching him in awe with their tongues hanging out. It was quite obvious that all was forgotten and Romeo was definitely back in the gang.

The Spikers, meanwhile, formed a tight closed circle near the beach volleyball court and practised war cries. Trembling with adrenaline and nerves, they shouted at the tops of their voices. And then they all leaped in the air and did a grand finale of high-fives. They were ready for the Dune High Decoys.

"Let's get something to drink before the game starts," suggested Nicks.

Coral nodded. And then she spied Zephyr and Sam walking side by side, joined at the elbow. They appeared lost in their conversation, as if the rest of the *Farewell to Summer* partygoers had ceased to exist. The girls tiptoed past. As experts in the field of love they knew better than to disturb a romance in progress. They would leave their dangling heart-shaped decorations to do their job instead.

Suddenly there was a loud, slow and steady clapping sound. The girls turned to discover that the Dune High Decoys had just arrived. Sunday Harbour folk were a sporting sort; of course they clapped the arrival of their opponents. The Spikers didn't look quite as friendly though. They clenched their jaws and stared at their rivals without flinching. A whistle blew. The two teams shook hands. Then it was game on.

Uh·huh

The Spikers were one point down with only eleven minutes to go. The girls watched from the sidelines and writhed in agony. It was almost excruciating to watch. *After everything, could it really come to this?*

The Sunday Harbour cheerleaders shook their pom-poms manically and cheered louder than ever before. As cheerleader captain, Cecily seemed to have forgotten her no-boyfriend troubles and led the group proudly in song. She really was very good. But the Decoys were not put off. One of their players performed a spectacular jump serve. The ball travelled over the net, landing directly in between two Spikers, who just could not move quickly enough. They were now two points down with nine minutes of the game left.

Romeo may have been a first-time volleyball mascot, but with a dog's intuition he seemed to sense that the situation was not looking good. He paced up and down the sidelines and ground his teeth. When the Spikers paused and huddled for a quick mid-game conference, he saw his chance. Quick as a blur he raced into the centre of the huddle, barking and howling and furiously kicking up sand with his small white paws. He really was having none of it.

The Spikers returned to their positions looking changed. They were having none of it either. For the next seven minutes they ran, dived, caught, served, blocked and attacked. They earned two points back too. But a tie was not a win. And there were only two minutes remaining.

It was Em's turn to serve. It went over the net and was returned by a Decoy. Rory slammed it back over the net but still a Decoy player sent it home again. Jem was ready though. She saw the ball coming and, with perfect timing, launched herself high into the air. Her right arm reached for the sun and her fist hung suspended over the ball for what seemed like minutes but could not have been more than a second or two. And then, with all the strength inside her, she suddenly slammed her fist down on the ball. It shot across the net and landed like a meteor on the ground, almost burying itself in the sand and sending a fine grainy spray over the Decoys. Jem's spike had won the Spikers the game! The crowd erupted. Coral and Nicks jumped up and down and hugged each other. Romeo ran around and around in circles, chasing his tail for joy. The cheerleaders cheered and hooted. And the Spikers huffed and puffed and grinned.

J.T. was amongst the volleyball crowd. The girls had noticed him arrive not long before the end of the game. He hadn't done much except stand and watch, but with the volleyball display finally over he suddenly seemed to come to life. He started jogging on the spot, blowing loudly through his mouth and moving his arms like pistons. Then he performed a dramatic vertical flip and landed on his back in the sand, where he proceeded to do rigorous sit-ups. Changing positions, he did leg presses. The girls watched, mesmerised. *Was J.T. trying to win over the volleyball fans?* They moved closer for inspection, but one of the organisers reached J.T. before they did.

"Excuse me lad, are you OK?" asked the organiser.

J.T. patted his midriff, *pat-pat*. "Oh yah,

226

sure! I'm in training for the Olympics. I'm a triathlete – running, swimming and cycling. I work out – it's my thing."

The organiser's eyes narrowed. "Uh, OK then. But don't go doing yourself an injury now." And then he shrugged and ambled back over to the organisers' tent.

Coral nudged Nicks in the ribs. "Look – there's Grace from the Beach Patrol."

"I'm almost too scared to look," replied Nicks. "Is she with Harry?"

Coral scanned the area but could not see Harry anywhere. And then suddenly he appeared, carrying two ice creams. He walked straight up to Grace and gave her a cone as well as a big kiss on her lips. "Yes! Yes! They've just kissed!"

"The Cupid Company definitely makes love relationships that are built to last," cheered Nicks.

Both girls smiled and stared ahead blissfully. It was good to see their old clients again.

This party was turning into a bit of a Cupid Company reunion, in fact. They were just about to walk over and say hello when Coral's mum appeared.

She gestured the girls to one side and pulled them into a secretive huddle. "Top secret info," she began. "Tamaran Lancaster is due to arrive at any moment."

"Ooooh!" cried the girls together.

"Shhh," replied Coral's mum as she glanced around. "There are plenty of girls here just dying to meet him. We cannot have the boy mobbed. But considering that you two really did so much to help with the party, I've arranged for you to be there when he arrives. Now come along quickly, we must hurry to the organisers' tent."

The girls did not waste a single precious moment – not even for a silent, best friend conversation. Besides, their faces really said it all. *They were going to meet Tamaran Lancaster!*

Slipping inside the cool shadow of the organisers' tent, they blinked a few times while their eyes adjusted. Inside there were two long trestle tables – one laden with cold drinks and paper plates piled with different kinds of biscuits. The other table had all sorts of papers and pamphlets and scattered pencils on its surface. Organisers with badges milled about and nibbled biscuits and nattered. Nobody seemed especially busy or excited. Coral glanced impatiently over to her mum. *So where was Tamaran Lancaster?*

Suddenly a voice announced: "He's here!" It set the organisers in motion, although none of them seemed to do anything in particular. And then the rear flap of the tent opened. A large triangle of sunlight pierced the tent's shade.

A large man dressed in black wearing sunglasses and an earpiece entered first. He scanned the tent's interior with an intimidating scowl. And then he spoke into a walkie-talkie.

This seemed to cue the arrival of a tall, thin man in a brown suit. Even when he stopped walking he was still moving. He announced that he was Tamaran's agent and that the star himself would be along at any moment. Then he tapped his mobile phone nervously and checked his pockets. Smoothing his hair, he traced his eyebrows with his fingertips before checking his pockets once again, consulting his watch and double-checking the time on his mobile phone. And then Tamaran Lancaster appeared.

He entered the tent like an angel with a halo – backlit by the bright sunshine outside as he waded into the shade. His hair was dark and tousled with gel and his eyes flashed as he stood there with his hands buried deep in his jeans pockets. His cheeky grin matched his T-shirt. It spelled: WISE GUY. He was definitely the coolest seventeen-year-old the girls had ever seen. *Like ever, in their entire lives.*

"It's good to be back in Sunday Harbour,"

he finally said in a voice that was like chocolate mousse. The girls licked their lips and stared ahead, mesmerised.

Coral's mum appeared and pressed a hand into the smalls of their backs, propelling the girls forward in his direction. "If you don't say hello now you'll miss your chance," she hissed.

And then suddenly they were standing right in front of him. The girls continued to stare at Tamaran Lancaster. Their jaws trailed. He definitely had the greenest eyes in the world. They were standing so close to him it was possible to reach out and touch him. In fact, Coral did. The WISE GUY T-shirt was soft.

Tamaran did not seem to mind. He was cool and calm and still grinning. Perhaps he was in training for the big time, when he would have plenty of fans reaching out to touch him. "Do you girls live in Sunday Harbour?" he drawled.

"Uh-huh," confirmed Coral and Nicks.

Tamaran glanced around and sighed like he was admiring the views of Sunday Harbour (and not the inside of a clammy canvas tent). "Such a great place!" he said.

"Uh-huh," replied Coral and Nicks.

"Best waves. Best ice cream. Best people," added the soon-to-be big star.

"Uh-huh," agreed Coral and Nicks.

"And that's an, er, interesting waistcoat," he said directly to Coral.

"Uh-huh," agreed Coral.

"Anyway girls, nice to meet you. Now I've really got to prepare for the performance."

They grinned. "Uh-huh."

He left – sandwiched in between his silent bodyguard and fidgety agent. The girls stared after him, unmoving. They couldn't even manage a silent, best friend conversation. Instead, they stood and grinned while warm and fuzzy thoughts about Tamaran Lancaster filled their heads like an explosion of hearts.

Chests hammered and tummies twisted. Toes tingled and tongues tied. As the Cupid Company, they'd had plenty to do with love until now. They were practically professionals. But they'd never (never ever) fallen in love themselves. And it felt like they might never recover.

lights, love

The advantage to the theatre-in-the-round was that the audience really did get to enjoy excellent views all round. And because this particular theatre-in-the-round was outdoors and on the beach, everyone could bask in summer's last remaining sunshine and bury their bare toes in the sand to keep cool. The crowd hummed with excitement – the females in the audience seemed especially energised.

Coral and Nicks guessed that this had very little to do with the play's plot or script. Everyone was here to see Tamaran Lancaster, and now they'd met him they understood why.

"Oh no, look at Cecily," groaned Nicks, who was finally able to speak, now that Tamaran was no longer in view.

Coral turned away from the stage (which was not easy considering that Tamaran was about to make his grand entrance at any moment). She spied their Cupid Company client scowling and trying to swipe at a dangling heart decoration.

"Tamaran will cheer her up," replied Coral. "CECILY!" she hollered as she patted the small bit of empty space beside her.

Cecily mooched over and slumped into the empty space. "I prefer the cinema," she grumbled, mumbling something about 'holding hands in the dark'. But there was no time for reassurances because Tamaran had just arrived in a bodyguard and agent sandwich, although it was only Tamaran who climbed on stage. He was greeted by cheers and hoots and loud whoops. Everyone loved a (soon-to-be) celebrity, but the people of Sunday Harbour were also very proud of the fact that a local lad was about to make it big. Coral and Nicks gazed at him with blissful smiles frozen on their happy faces.

The cheering audience seemed to prick Cecily's interest. Her spine straightened and her creased brow softened. She turned her head this way and that as she stared at the excited audience in wonder. She glanced over at Tamaran. And then she turned back to the applauding audience before finally fixing her attention on Tamaran once more. Her face opened and her features lifted. She looked absolutely amazed. The girls watched her closely. And then it all became very clear.

Cecily was not taken by Tamaran. She was mesmerised by all the attention Tamaran

was receiving. Being the centre of attention really was one of Cecily's favourite things in the world!

Tamaran waved to the audience and planted kisses in his cupped hands which he then released into the air as if they were doves. The audience cried out even louder than before. Cecily stared at them all and smiled slowly, as if life finally made some sense to her. Tamaran, of course, knew none of this. He was too busy telling the audience that today he – along with the Sunday Harbour Theatre Company actors – would be improvising. This was a type of theatre where the actors – or improvisers – used audience suggestions to guide their performance. Nothing had been rehearsed and the actors would rely on each other to create the dialogue, setting and plot as they went along.

But there was still more. Today one lucky audience member would have the opportunity to take part in the performance.

Nicks leaned forward eagerly. Her hand shot up.

Cecily leaped to her feet at that exact same moment.

"CHOOSE CECILY!" Nicks cried out.

"PICK ME! PICK ME!" shouted Cecily.

The rest of the audience never stood a chance.

Tamaran chuckled at the two girls. "I guess it's between Cecily and uh–?"

"CECILY!" cried Cecily.

"Well, come on up then," replied Tamaran.

For a moment Cecily simply stood there. And then she plumped up her hair, adjusted her skirt and fixed the corners of her lip-glossed mouth. Finally, she was ready.

"Excuse me, excuse me," she cooed as she zigzagged through the audience. She finally made it through and Tamaran helped her up on stage.

"Everyone please give a warm welcome to Cecily!" he insisted.

And everyone did. They clapped and cheered. Cecily was captivated. Her smile grew and grew until it was almost big enough to see from the moon. She gazed out happily at the rows of people who were all cheering... *for her.*

The rest of the improvisers appeared on stage and the audience was just as welcoming. Not that Cecily noticed; she was too busy twirling on the spot.

"Now we need you to suggest a theme for our performance," Tamaran said to the audience.

"The end of summer!" shouted one.

Tamaran turned to the rest of the improvisers. "The end of summer it is." And then the group had a quick huddled discussion and each claimed a character. Cecily formed part of the huddle, but kept stepping out and waving to the audience with a silly smile on her face.

The girls watched closely. "She really

should be paying attention," said Nicks worriedly.

"She'll be OK," murmured Coral, who was still smiling and staring at Tamaran.

Nicks focused on Tamaran too. "Mmm, yes, you're probably right…" she replied dreamily.

The group of improvisers scattered and the action got underway. Tamaran was playing the part of a professional surfer who had lost an arm in a shark attack. He was very good and still very handsome, even with only one arm.

It was not quite as easy to work out which part Cecily was playing, who was strolling around the stage winking at the audience.

"Maybe she lost an eye in the shark attack?" suggested Coral.

Then Cecily strolled less and paused at intervals in front of different sections of the audience where she struck poses and battered her eyelashes.

"Perhaps she's one of those beach beauty contestants?" offered Nicks. "You know, like Miss Bikini or something."

Suddenly there was another shark attack and Tamaran lay fighting for his life on the stage floor.

"Two shark attacks really is terrible luck," commented Coral. "Perhaps he should switch to land sports."

Cecily finally seemed to notice the commotion the dying Tamaran was causing. Or perhaps she noticed that Tamaran had claimed all of the audience's attention. She flitted over to where he lay face down and suddenly raised her hands in the air as if holding imaginary pom-poms. She jumped high and began swinging alternate legs in the air while chanting:

"Hip, hip,
Boom, boom, bah,
F – I – G – H – T
A fighter is what you are!

Siss, siss,

Ooh, ooh, ow,

D – O – N - T

Don't die now!"

Nobody spoke a word. The only sound was the whistle of the wind. And then Tamaran lifted his head. He stared up at Cecily with a quizzical sort of look.

"You know, I don't think she's playing any particular character," observed Nicks dryly, "I think she's just being Cecily."

Finally the audience started clapping, although it was in a faltering, confused sort of way. There was, however, one fan who seemed very convinced by Cecily's performance. J.T. stood up in his seat and made loud 'WHOO HOO' sounds. He waved his muscular arms and clapped louder and more determinedly than anyone else. It was quite clear he thought Cecily was something special – that, like him, she was the sort who would go far in life and stand out from the crowd.

Cecily did not seem to mind the audience's mixed response. She tittered and waved to the fans. And then her eyes found Coral and Nicks in the audience. She shrieked and gave them a thumbs-up signal, as if to say: *this is far better than any boyfriend!*

24

a summer of love

The sun seemed to hang directly over Sunday Harbour for a little longer than usual that day before it began its slow, steady slide down the blue, cloudless sky. Dusk was just as impressive, streaking the sky pink and red to match the flames of the bonfire which had just been lit. But it was still the sand lady who captured most people's attention. She stood almost five feet tall, and she was not quite finished yet. She was the colour of damp beach sand and had a squat body and a large round head resting on her broad shoulders. Coral and Nicks stood back and eyed her critically. She actually looked more like a sand yeti, but a few clever accessories would soon change that.

"How about a necklace..." murmured Coral thoughtfully as she reached for a string of foil hearts that had been hanging as decoration.

Nicks grinned and removed the grips with heart-shaped tips from her hair. "You can't have a necklace without matching earrings," she said.

Somebody pressed a pair of white-framed sunglasses to the sand lady's face and another person gave her lips made out of bright red liquorice laces. Three small children giggled and wedged a pair of rubber flip-flops into her base so that just the front half of the shoes stuck out.

"Here, she'd better have my straw hat," said a mum with a toddler on her hip.

"Hold on," said Cecily, who had just appeared. She turned and smiled at the crowd like she owed it to them and then added one of her cheerleading pom-poms to the sand lady's head before the toddler's mum could add her hat. "There – a perfect head of hair," she announced as she waved to everyone like a film star.

"And sticks for arms," said a boy who was dragging a polystyrene boogie board transporting pebbles, shells and the rest of the paraphernalia he'd recently found on the beach. Romeo stared at the sand lady, sniffed the air and suddenly raced off. He soon returned with a mouthful of wild flowers he'd picked from the sand dunes.

Coral patted the panting pup's head. "Flowers for her hat – excellent work!" she said.

"And a wafer cone for a nose," added

Mr Gelatti, who had been watching from his ice cream stall nearby.

"You're welcome to this – if you can use it," said a lifesaver. He was holding what looked like a large piece of shiny silver material. "It's a foil emergency blanket," he added sheepishly.

Coral and Nicks smiled and artfully draped the emergency blanket around the sand lady, who now looked rather dazzling and nothing like a yeti whatsoever. People started clapping and cheering. Their sand lady really was the perfect tribute to the perfect summer.

Nicks leaned over and yelled above the cheering. "Look there – it's Malcolm and Meredith!"

Coral spied their old beach hut neighbours and Cupid Company clients straight away. The pair touched shoulders and laughed together as they strolled. They looked happier than ever.

"I wonder what's brought them back to Sunday Harbour?" Coral asked Nicks.

"Do you think they're here to buy the red beach hut? I mean, it is for sale and they did love the place very much."

The girls both considered this for a moment. Of course it would be brilliant to have Malcolm and Meredith back again. The couple had only rented the red beach hut next door for a short while, but still the girls felt like they were old friends. And yet that would mean saying goodbye to Zephyr. Poor old Zephyr. Poor old Sam. They'd only just found each other. Was it all over before it had even properly begun?

"Ooooh!" cried a new voice on the scene. The girls turned to find Zephyr standing there looking mesmerised. She reached out and stroked the shiny material of the foil emergency blanket like it was magic. She then stepped back to admire the sand lady and whistled loudly. "Oh, Amor and Pixie, believe me when I say that this really is a most perfect outfit!"

Coral chuckled. "I'm sure you can have the foil emergency blanket when the sand lady is through with it." And then she noticed Sam, who had just sidled up close to Zephyr. Sam had noticed Coral too. He stared at her waistcoat with eyes that were misty with remembering. Of course Zephyr knew nothing of the waistcoat's history. She was clearly still taken with the sand lady's foil dress and soon found herself drawn back to its silver shininess. But Sam didn't budge.

"I never thought I'd see that thing again..." he said with a fond sigh. "It was given to me by a very special lady. I always wore it on opening night and it brought us luck every time."

"Why did you give it up?" asked Nicks.

"We were raising money for the theatre after our leading lady, Cybil B. Arcadia, moved away in search of a bigger, brighter spotlight. And well, she'd been my leading lady too. But I had to get on with my life... everything had changed. Donating that waistcoat seemed like the best thing to do," Sam replied distractedly. "I felt like I'd lost everything that mattered to me anyway."

"Actually, we have something that is still yours," said Coral. She reached for the lucky penny and passed it to Sam who stared at it, surprised.

"My lucky penny – I thought I'd lost it somewhere."

"Well, we thought you'd like it back."

"How did you know it was mine in the firs—"

But Nicks just waved her hand in the air. "That's the thing about a lucky penny – it's lucky." The girls grinned.

Zephyr managed to drag herself away from the silver dress and returned to Sam's side, nestling in close. Sam remained serious for a few moments and then finally he smiled too.

"You must keep the penny," he said firmly. "It's yours now."

Coral and Nicks were about to protest but

Sam frowned. "Now, now, girls, that lucky penny is *yours*." And then he turned to Zephyr. His pretend frown transformed into a genuine smile. "Besides, I don't think I have any use for it now. I think I have all the good luck and happiness I need." Zephyr matched his knowing smile. It was like they shared a secret nobody else knew about, but they weren't letting on.

The sun finally left the sky, taking most of its warmth with it. The people of Sunday Harbour quickly moved on from the sand lady and edged closer to the bonfire, which seemed alive. Its red and gold fingers reached for the stars and the huddled faces glowed orange, almost as if they'd been licked by flames. Every now and again somebody stepped forward to add more wood to the fire and it wasn't long before small children fell soundly asleep in parents' laps. Everyone looked warm and happy and at peace beneath the stars, surrounded by hearts.

"There you girls are." It was Nicks's mum. Of course Ben and Miss Honey were with her. Romeo quickly edged closer to Coral and promptly fell into a deep fake-sleep. Miss Honey just huffed through her nose.

"We've been looking for you," said Ben.

"It's been a busy day," replied Coral with a satisfied smile on her face.

"It's been a *great* day," added Nicks's mum. "And a great summer. Still, I can't wait for autumn. And winter too."

"You can't?" replied Nicks.

"We all have so much to look forward to," continued her mum. "I have my new teaching job. You have a new school term. Ben has the penguin chicks."

Ben reached out and draped an arm across the girls' shoulders. "I certainly do have the penguin chicks to look forward to – thanks to you two." He then pulled Nicks just a little closer to his side. "And there's something even more special to look forward to. Miss

Honey and I really hope that we can all spend more time together... you know, as a family."

Coral straightened at the sound of Miss Honey's name. "Erm, Romeo will be very busy with mascot duties..." she began. Then she saw Nicks place an arm around Ben. Her friend was smiling and looked quite contented, as if all her anxieties had finally disappeared. So Coral kept quiet and smiled too. *It would be good if Nicks and her mum and Ben could be a family.*

Suddenly there was the sound of clapping. They turned towards the sound. Zephyr was marching towards the bonfire with a large FOR SALE sign in her hand. She stopped short of the bonfire and tossed the sign into its dancing flames. She then turned to face the cheering crowd. Backlit by the fire, her face was in shadow, but the girls still noticed her swipe a shiny tear from the corner of her eye.

"Home sweet home!" she cried out happily.

Everyone cheered some more, but no one

louder than Sam. The girls beamed. It looked like another score for the Cupid Company and true love! They were still beaming when Zephyr slipped in between the two girls and elbowed them playfully in the ribs. "I hope this town is big enough for *three* matchmakers," she said.

"Three?" Nicks gulped.

Zephyr grinned. "Well, I am getting quite a reputation for matchmaking – *animals*, that is." The girls chuckled and Zephyr continued. "I can't wait to sort those penguins out."

"And when you're done with the penguins," replied Coral, "perhaps you could find Miss Honey a new boyfriend?"

Zephyr nodded and grinned. "Anything for my wonderful beach hut neighbours, Amor and Binksie."

Nicks coughed. "Actually, you'd better call me Venus."

"VENUS?" Coral almost choked on the word.

"Sure – I could go for this exotic name thing

254

too. If it works for Tamaran Lancaster, then it works for me."

Zephyr clapped. "Venus – the Roman goddess of love and beauty – how marvellous and utterly memorable!"

"The Roman goddess of love and beauty...?" mumbled Coral. Suddenly Amor did not sound nearly exotic enough.

Just then Cecily marched by with her legs and elbows flying. She waved to people as she passed, but she smiled through gritted teeth. "Euugh, the fans!" they heard her mutter furiously.

And then they saw him. J.T. was chasing after Cecily. He stumbled, got up from his knees and pressed on wearily. "Come back, Cecily," he cried feebly, "you know we're special... we're not like everyone else..."

Nicks shook her head. "Summer may be over but somebody still needs to rescue that boy. Come on, Cupid Company!"

Romeo yapped and wagged his tail. But

Coral was still staring at the ground, lost in thought. "Amor... it's just not exotic enough..." she mumbled.

Nicks chuckled. "Here, this might help to take your mind off things," she said, handing her best friend the long, slender roll of paper she'd been hiding behind her back.

"What is it?"

"Open it."

Coral removed the elastic band from the roll and watched the paper unfurl. It was one of the promotional posters featuring Tamaran Lancaster – full-size and in colour. Romeo dropped to the sand and placed his paws over his eyes. Coral shuffled up to Nicks and rested her head on her shoulder. Both girls stared ahead into the distance and sighed out loud.

"He'll look good in Coral Hut."

"He'll be our inspiration."

It certainly had been a summer of love. The girls of the Cupid Company would never be the same again.